"So it's true?"

Leonidas's voice was dangerously low, his black eyes gleaming like white-hot coals in the twilight. He looked down at her belly, bulging out beneath the long, puffy black coat. "You're pregnant?"

Instinctively, she wrapped her hands over her baby bump. There was no way to deny it. How had he heard? She trembled all over. "What are you doing here?"

"Are you, Daisy?"

She could hardly deny it. "Yes."

His burning gaze met hers. "Is the baby mine?"

She swallowed hard, wanting more than anything to lie. But she couldn't. Even though Leonidas had lied to her about his identity, and lied about Daisy's father, she couldn't fall to his level. She couldn't lie to his face. Not even for her child. What kind of mother would she be if she practiced the same deceit as Leonidas Niarxos?

USA TODAY bestselling author **Jennie Lucas**'s parents owned a bookstore, so she grew up surrounded by books, dreaming about faraway lands. A fourth-generation Westerner, she went east at sixteen to boarding school on a scholarship, wandered the world, got married, then finally worked her way through college before happily returning to her hometown. A 2010 RITA® Award finalist and 2005 Golden Heart® Award winner, she lives in Idaho with her husband and children.

Books by Jennie Lucas

Harlequin Presents

Christmas Baby for the Greek
Her Boss's One-Night Baby
Claiming the Virgin's Baby

Conveniently Wed!

Chosen as the Sheikh's Royal Bride

One Night With Consequences

Claiming His Nine-Month Consequence

Secret Heirs of Billionaires

Carrying the Spaniard's Child

Secret Heirs and Scandalous Brides

The Secret the Italian Claims
The Heir the Prince Secures
The Baby the Billionaire Demands

Visit the Author Profile page
at Harlequin.com for more titles.

Jennie Lucas

—

PENNILESS AND
SECRETLY PREGNANT

HARLEQUIN®
PRESENTS®

Recycling programs
for this product may
not exist in your area.

ISBN-13: 978-1-335-89405-2

Penniless and Secretly Pregnant

Copyright © 2020 by Jennie Lucas

For questions and comments about the quality of this book,
please contact us at CustomerService@Harlequin.com.

Harlequin Enterprises ULC
22 Adelaide St. West, 40th Floor
Toronto, Ontario M5H 4E3, Canada
www.Harlequin.com

Printed in U.S.A.

PENNILESS AND
SECRETLY PREGNANT

To Pete—Then, Now and Always

CHAPTER ONE

HE COULDN'T AVOID it any longer. He had to tell her the truth.

From the bed, Leonidas Niarxos looked out the window. Across the river, on the other side of the bridge, Manhattan skyscrapers twinkled in the violet and pink sunrise.

Taking a deep breath, he looked down at the woman sleeping in his arms. For the last four weeks, he'd enjoyed the most exhilarating affair of his life. After years of brief, meaningless relationships with women who had hearts as cold as his own, Daisy Cassidy had been like a fire. Warming him. *Burning him.*

For weeks now—from their very first, accidental, surprising night—he'd been promising himself he would end their affair. He would tell her who he really was.

But he'd put it off, always wanting one more day. Even now, after a night of lovemaking, Leonidas wanted her. As he looked at her, feeling her soft naked body pressed so trustingly against his,

his willpower weakened. Perhaps he could put off his confession one more day. Until tomorrow.

No, he thought furiously. No!

He had to end this. Daisy was falling in love with him. He'd seen it in her lovely face, in her heartbreakingly luminous green eyes. She believed Leonidas to be Leo Gianakos, a decent, kind-hearted man. Perfect, she called him. She thought he was a store clerk without a penny to his name.

Lies, all lies.

Maybe if he took her to his house in Manhattan first, it might soften the blow, he argued with himself. Maybe Daisy would be more likely to forgive him in his fifty-million-dollar mansion, while he offered her a life filled with luxury and glamour...

Forget it. Did he really believe that either love or money would make Daisy forgive what he'd done? After he revealed his real name, the only emotions she'd ever feel for him again would be horror and hate.

It had all been stolen time.

She sighed in his arms. Looking down, he saw her dark eyelashes flutter in the gray dawn.

He had to tell her. Now. Get it over with. For her sake. For his own.

"Daisy," he said quietly. "Are you awake?"

Stretching her limbs out luxuriously between the soft cotton sheets, Daisy blinked dreamily in the pale light of dawn. Her naked body was filled with the sweet ache of another night of lovemaking. She felt delicious. She felt cherished. She felt like she was in love.

Was she also in trouble?

Her eyes flew open. *You don't* know *anything's wrong*, she told herself fiercely. *It might be nothing. It* has *to be nothing.*

But her ridiculous fear had already ruined their date last night, when Leo had gone to tremendous expense to take her to a way too fancy French restaurant in Williamsburg. She'd been miserable—not just afraid of using the wrong fork, not just uncomfortable in the formal setting, but haunted by a new, awful suspicion.

Could she be pregnant?

"Daisy?" Leo's voice was a husky growl, his powerful body exuding heat and strength as he wrapped one muscular arm around her in the large bed.

"Good morning." Pushing away her fears, she smiled up at his darkly handsome face, silhouetted by the rising dawn.

He hesitated. "How did you sleep?"

Daisy gave him a shyly wicked grin. *"Sleep?"*

Leo gave her an answering grin, and his gaze fell slowly to her lips, her throat, her breasts barely covered by the sheet clinging to her nipples. Over the sheet, his hand brushed her belly, and she wondered again if she could be pregnant.

No. She couldn't be. They'd used protection, even that first wild night four weeks ago, when he'd taken her virginity.

But as he softly stroked her body, her breasts felt strangely tender, swollen, beneath his sensual hands...

A sigh rose from the back of his throat as Leo reluctantly pulled away. "Daisy, we need to talk."

Never a phrase anyone wanted to hear. She swallowed. Did her body feel different to him? Had he already guessed her fear? "Talk about what?"

"There's something I need to tell you," he said in a low voice. "Something you're not going to like."

His grim black eyes met hers, over his cruel, sensual mouth and hard jaw, dark with five o'clock shadow.

An awful new fear exploded in the back of her mind.

How much did she really know about him?

After a hellish year, Leo Gianakos had wandered into her life last month like a miracle, like a dream, all dark eyes, tanned skin, sharp cheekbones and a million-dollar smile. From the moment Daisy had first looked at his breathtaking masculine beauty, at his powerful shoulders in that perfectly tailored suit, she'd known he was a thousand miles out of her league.

Yet somehow, they'd ended up in bed. Since

that magical day, they'd spent nearly every night together, whenever she wasn't at work.

But it was strange to realize how little she actually knew about him. She didn't know where he worked, or where he lived. He'd always evaded personal questions.

There were all kinds of good reasons why, she'd told herself. Perhaps Leo shared a tiny rat-infested studio with three roommates and was self-conscious about it. After all, not everyone had a wealthy artist friend, as Daisy did, who'd asked them to house-sit. If not for Franck's generosity, Daisy would undoubtedly be sharing a studio with three people, too.

She hadn't pushed Leo for details about his life. They were happy; that was enough.

Now, for the first time, a horrible idea occurred to her. Could there be some other, more sinister reason why he hadn't told her where he worked, or invited her to his apartment? What if—could he possibly be—

"Are you married?" she blurted out, her heart in her throat.

Leo blinked, then gave a low laugh. "Married? If I were married, could I be here in bed with you?"

"Well, are you?" she said stubbornly.

He snorted, his black eyes glinting. "No. I am not married. And for the record, I don't ever intend to be. Ever." His voice dropped to a husky whisper. "That's not the problem."

Daisy stared at him. She was relieved he wasn't married, but...

Leo didn't want to get married? Ever?

She took a deep breath. "I just know so little about you," she said in a small voice. "I don't know where you work, or where you live. I've never met your family or friends."

Pulling away from her, Leo pushed off the sheets and abruptly stood up from the bed. She enjoyed the vision of his powerful naked body in the rosy morning light. She drank in the image of his muscular backside, the strong muscles of his back.

Without looking at her, he reached down to the floor, and started putting on his clothes. Finally, as he pulled on his shirt, he turned back to face her. She was distracted by the brief vision of his muscular chest, laced with dark hair, before he buttoned up the shirt. He looked down at her. "Do you really want to see where I live? Does it matter so much?"

"Of course it matters!" Sitting up in bed, holding the sheet over her breasts with one hand, she motioned around the spacious bedroom with its view of the Manhattan skyline. "Do you think I'd be living in a place like this if my dad's oldest friend hadn't taken pity on me? So please don't feel self-conscious, whatever your apartment is like. Or your job. Whatever it is, I will always think you're perfect!"

Leo stopped buttoning up his shirt. Dropping his hands to his sides, he stared at her across the bedroom, silhouetted by the view of the East River and Manhattan beyond.

She realized he was going to break up with her. She could see it in his grim expression, in the tightness of his sensual lips.

She'd always known this day would come. Leo was ten years older, sexy, tall, broad shouldered and darkly handsome. Daisy had never quite understood what he'd seen in her in the first place. She was so…ordinary. How could a badly dressed, not very interesting waitress from Brooklyn possibly keep the attention of a man like Leo Gianakos?

And if she was pregnant…

No. She couldn't be. *Couldn't.*

Leo took a deep breath. "Would you like to come to my house? Right now? And then…we can talk."

His voice was so strained, it took several seconds for Daisy to realize he was inviting her to his apartment, not breaking up with her.

"Sure." She realized she was smiling.

No, quick, don't let him see; he can't know I'm falling in love with him.

It had been only a month. Even Daisy, with her total lack of romantic experience, knew it was too soon to confess her feelings. Turning her face away, she rose from the bed. "I'll go take a shower…"

She felt Leo's gaze follow her as she walked naked across the luxurious bedroom. Entering the lavish en suite bathroom, she tossed him back a single glance.

Before she'd even had time to turn on the water in the enormous walk-in shower, Leo had caught up with her, already rapidly pulling off his clothes. He kissed her passionately as she pulled away from him with a light laugh, drawing him into the hot, steamy water. They washed each other, and he stroked every inch of her. She leaned back her head as he washed her long brown hair. After she'd rinsed, she straightened, and saw the dark heat of his gaze.

Pushing her against the hot, wet tiled wall, he kissed her, and she nearly gasped as her sensitive, swollen nipples brushed against his muscular chest, laced with rough dark hair. She felt the hardness of him pushing against her soft belly, and yearned. Finally, he wrenched away from her with a rueful growl. "No condom," he sighed.

As he turned off the water, and gently toweled her off with the thick cotton towels, in the back of her mind Daisy wondered nervously if it was already too late for that, if she could be pregnant in spite of their precautions.

Taking her hand in his own, he pulled her back

to the bed and made love to her, gently, tenderly, after a night during which they'd already made love twice. She told herself it was their lovemaking which caused her breasts to feel so heavy, her nipples so sensitive that she gasped as he suckled her. That had to be the reason. There could be lots of reasons why her cycle, normally so predictable, was two weeks late… She couldn't be pregnant. *Couldn't.*

She pushed the thought away as Leo lightly kissed her cheeks, her forehead. Smoothing back her unruly brown hair, he cupped her jawline with his powerful hands, and lowered his lips to hers. His kiss was hot and sweet against her lips, so, so sweet, and she was lost in the breathless grip of desire. As he pushed inside her, she cried out with pleasure, soaring to new heights before he, too, exploded.

Afterward, Leo held her tight against his powerful body, the white cotton sheets twisted at their feet. Blinking fast, Daisy stared out the window toward the unforgiving Manhattan skyline, and heard the grim echo of his words.

I am not married. And for the record, I don't ever intend to be. Ever.

His hands tightened around her. "I don't want to lose you," he said in a low voice.

"Lose me?" She peeked at him in bed. "Why would you?"

He gave a low laugh. It had no humor in it. "Let's go to my house. And talk."

"Talk about what?"

"About…me." His serious expression as he got dressed sent panic through her. Nervously, she pulled on clothes in turn, a clean T-shirt and jeans.

"I'm not scheduled to work today. Are you?"

"I can be late," he said flatly.

"Don't clerks need to be at the store when it opens at ten?" When he didn't respond, she tried again. "You won't be fired if you're late?"

"Fired?" Leo sounded grimly amused. "No." He gave her a smile that didn't meet his eyes. "Shall we go?"

As they left the apartment, he held the door open for her, as usual. He was always gallant that way, making her feel cherished and cared for.

When she was younger, and even now that she was twenty-four, boys her age always seemed to want quick, meaningless hookups, without bothering with old-fashioned niceties like opening doors, bringing flowers, giving compliments or even showing up on time. No wonder Daisy had been a virgin when she met Leo. Ten years older, powerful, and handsome like a Greek god, no wonder she'd fallen into bed with him the first night!

Now, as they left the co-op building, going out into the fresh October morning, Daisy glanced at him out of the corner of her eye. She should have been thrilled he was taking her to his apartment. Instead, she had a weird sense of foreboding. What did Leo want to talk about? And which of her own secrets might tumble from her mouth— her love for him, her possible pregnancy or even the fact that she was the daughter of a convicted felon?

As they walked, sunshine sparkled across the East River with the enormous bridge and Manhattan skyline beyond. She started to head for the nearest subway entrance, two blocks away, when he stopped her.

"Let's take a car."

He seemed strangely tense. Smiling, she shook her head. "You can't seriously want to get a rideshare, after all the expense of that fancy dinner last night. The subway is fine. You don't need to bankrupt yourself trying to impress me." She couldn't help thinking how much she loved him for trying. "You're already perfect."

"I didn't mean a rideshare."

She heard a noise behind him. Frowning, she tilted her head. "Did you hear that?"

"Hear what?"

She looked around. "Sounds like a baby crying."

"I'm sure there are children everywhere here. Its mother will take care of it."

A baby was an *it*? Daisy's forehead furrowed.

Then she heard the soft cry again. Weak. More like a whine, or a snuffle. She turned toward the alley behind the gleaming waterfront co-op.

"Where are you going?" he asked.

"I just need to make sure…"

"Daisy, it's not your problem—"

But she was already hurrying toward the alley, following the sound. There had been a newspaper story just the month before about a baby abandoned in an alley in New Jersey. Thankfully that child had been found safely, but Daisy couldn't get the story out of her mind. If she didn't investigate this, and something bad happened…

She followed the sound down the alley and was only vaguely aware of Leo behind her. She saw a burlap bag resting on the top of a dumpster. The sound seemed to come from that. It was wiggling. She heard a weak whine. Then a whimper.

"Daisy, don't," Leo said sharply behind her. "You don't know what it is."

But she was already reaching for the bag. It weighed almost nothing. Setting the burlap bag gently on the asphalt, she undid the tie and opened it.

It was a tiny puppy, a fuzzy golden-colored mutt, maybe two months old, wiggling and crying. She stroked it tenderly. "It's a dog!" Sudden rage filled Daisy. "Who would leave a puppy in a dumpster?"

"People can be monsters," Leo said flatly. She

looked back at him, bemused. Then the puppy whined, weakly licking her hand, taking all her attention.

"She seems all right," Daisy said anxiously, petting the animal. "But I'd better take her to the vet to make sure." She looked up at Leo. "Do you want to come?"

He looked grim. "To the vet? No."

"I'm so sorry. Could we maybe get together later? You could show me your apartment tonight?"

"Tonight?" His jaw set. "I'm having a party."

She brightened. "How fun! I'd love to meet your friends."

"Fine," he said shortly. "I'll send a car to pick you up at seven."

"I told you, a car's not necessary—"

"Wear a cocktail dress," he cut her off.

"All right." Daisy tried to remember if she even owned a cocktail dress. Carrying the puppy carefully in her arms, she reached up on her tiptoes and kissed Leo's scratchy cheek. "Thanks for understanding. I'll see you at your party."

"Daisy—"

"What?"

She waited, but he didn't continue. He finally said in a strangled voice, "See you tonight."

And he turned away. She watched him stride down the street, his hands pushed in his pockets. Why was he acting so weird? Was he really so embarrassed of where he lived? Embarrassed of his friends?

She looked down at the puppy in her arms, who whined weakly. Turning on her heel, she hurried down the street, going to the veterinary office owned by one of her father's old friends.

"Dr. Lopez, please," she panted, "it's an emergency…"

The kindly veterinarian took one look at the tiny animal in Daisy's arms and waved her inside his office. After an exam, she was relieved to hear the mixed breed puppy was slightly dehydrated, but otherwise fine.

"Someone must have just wanted to get rid of her. She must have been dumped sometime during the night," Dr. Lopez said. "It's lucky the weather isn't colder, or else…"

Daisy shivered. It was heartbreaking to think that while she'd been snuggled warm in bed in Leo's arms, some awful person had been dumping an innocent puppy in the alley, leaving her to die in a burlap bag.

People can be monsters. Leo was right. All Daisy had to do was remember those awful lawyers who'd vindictively harassed her innocent father into prison on those trumped-up forgery charges. Her tenderhearted, artistic-minded father had collapsed in prison, surrounded by strangers. He'd had a stroke and died—

"What are you going to name her?" the vet

asked, mercifully pulling her from her thoughts. Daisy blinked.

"Me?"

"Sure, she's your dog now, isn't she?"

Daisy looked down at the puppy on the examining table. She couldn't possibly own a pet. She didn't even rent her own apartment. Franck Bain was due to return from Europe soon, and she'd need to find a new place to live. With her meager income, it was unlikely she'd be able to afford an apartment that allowed a pet. Just thinking of the cost in dog food alone—

No. Daisy couldn't keep her.

But someone had left this puppy to starve. A sweet floppy mutt who just needed a loving home. Could Daisy really abandon her?

Uncertainly, she reached out and softly stroked the dog's head. The animal's big dark eyes looked up at her, and she licked Daisy's hand with a tiny rough tongue.

No. She couldn't.

"You're right. I'm keeping her." She pushed away the worry of expensive vet bills and dog food. "I'll think about a name."

Dr. Lopez tried to wave off her offer of payment, but she insisted on paying. She couldn't live off the charity of her father's friends forever. It was bad enough she'd lived in Franck's apartment for so long, even if he insisted *she* was the one doing him a favor by house-sitting.

She wondered if the gray-haired artist would still think so, after he discovered she'd brought a puppy home.

Leaving the vet's, she went to the nearest bodega and bought puppy food and other pet supplies. Passing another aisle in the store, she hesitated, then furtively added a pregnancy test into her basket, too. Just so she could prove her fears were ridiculous.

After Daisy got the puppy back home and fed, she stroked her fur. "How could anyone have thrown you away?" she whispered. "You're perfect." Finally, gathering her courage, she left the tiny dog to drowse on the fluffy rug in front of the gas fire and went into the elegant modern bathroom to take the pregnancy test. *Just get it over with*, she told herself. Once she took the test, she would be able to relax.

Instead, she found out to her shock her fears were right.

She was pregnant.

Pregnant by a man she loved, though she barely knew him.

Pregnant by a man who would never marry her.

Daisy didn't have any money. She didn't have a permanent home. She didn't have a family. Soon, she'd be raising both a puppy and a baby, utterly alone.

She couldn't do it alone. She *couldn't*.

Could she?

She had to tell Leo at the party tonight. The idea terrified her. What would he do when he found out she was pregnant? What would he say? Fear gripped Daisy as she looked at herself in the bathroom mirror.

What had she done by following her heart?

Leonidas Niarxos was in a foul mood as he arrived at his skyscraper in Midtown Manhattan, the headquarters of his international luxury conglomerate, Liontari Inc.

"Good morning, Mr. Niarxos."

"Good morning, sir."

Various employees greeted him as he stalked through the enormous lobby. Then they took one look at his wrathful face and promptly fled. Even his longtime chauffeur, Jenkins, who'd picked him up in Brooklyn—around the corner from Daisy's building, so she wouldn't see the incriminating Rolls-Royce—had known better than to speak as he'd driven his boss back across the Manhattan Bridge. Leonidas was simmering, brooking for a fight. But he had only himself to blame.

He hadn't been able to tell Daisy his real name.

She'd looked at him with her mesmerizing green eyes, her sensual body barely covered by a sheet, and she'd hinted that seeing where Leonidas lived might make a difference—might give them a future.

At least, that was what he'd wanted to hear. So he'd given in to the temptation to postpone his confession. He'd convinced himself that pleading his case in the private luxury of his mansion, later, after he'd made love to her one last time, might lead to a different outcome.

Now he was paying for that choice. Leonidas Niarxos, billionaire playboy CEO, had just been upstaged by a dog. And he would be forced to confess his true identity in the middle of a political fundraiser, surrounded by the ruthless, powerful people he called friends. Besides, did he honestly think, no matter where or when he told Daisy the truth, she'd ever forgive what he'd done?

Standing alone in his private elevator, Leonidas gritted his teeth, and pushed the button for the top floor.

Daisy was different from any woman he'd ever met. She loved everyone and hid nothing. Her emotions shone on her face, on her body. Joy and tenderness. Desire and need. Her warmth and goodness, her kindness and innocent sensuality, had made him feel alive as he'd never felt before. She'd even been a virgin when he'd first made love to her. How was it possible?

Leonidas never should have sought her out a month ago. But then, he'd never imagined they would fall into an affair. Especially since he'd sent her father to prison.

A year ago, Leonidas had heard a small-time Brooklyn art dealer had somehow procured *Love with Birds*, the Picasso he'd desperately sought for two decades. His lawyer, Edgar Ross, had arranged for Leonidas to see it in his office.

But he'd known at first sight it was fake. He'd felt heartsick at yet another wild-goose chase, trying to recover the shattered loss of his childhood. He'd told his lawyer to press charges, then used his influence with the New York prosecutor to punish the hapless art dealer to the fullest extent of the law.

He'd found out later that the Brooklyn art dealer had been selling minor forgeries for years. His mistake had been trying to move up to the big leagues with a Picasso—and trying to sell it to Leonidas Niarxos.

The old man's trial had become a New York sensation. Leonidas never attended the trial, but everyone had known he was behind it.

It was only later that Leonidas had regrets, especially after his lawyer had told him about the man's daughter, who'd loyally sat behind her elderly father in court, day after day, with huge eyes. He'd seen the daughter's stricken face in a poignant drawing of the courtroom, as she'd tearfully thrown her arms around her father when the verdict had come down and he'd been sentenced to six years. She'd clearly believed in Patrick Cassidy's innocence to the end.

A few months ago, on hearing the man had died suddenly in prison, Leonidas hadn't been able to shake a strange, restless guilt. As angry as he'd been at the man's deceit, even *he* didn't think death was the correct punishment for the crime of art forgery.

So last month, Leonidas had gone to the Brooklyn diner where Daisy Cassidy worked as a waitress, to confirm for himself the girl was all right, and anonymously leave her a ten-thousand-dollar tip.

Instead, as the pretty young brunette had served him coffee, eggs and bacon, they got to talking about art and movies and literature, and he was amazed at how fascinating she was, how funny, warm and kind. And so damn beautiful. Leonidas had lingered, finally asking her if she wanted to meet after her shift ended.

He'd lied to her.

No. He hadn't lied, not exactly. The name he'd given her was a nickname his nanny had given him in childhood, Leo, along with his patronymic, Gianakos.

Leo, Daisy called him, her voice so musical and light, and hearing that name on her sweet lips, he always felt like a different person. A better man.

No woman had ever affected him like this before. Why now? Why her?

He'd never intended to seduce her. But Daisy's warmth and innocent sensuality had been like fire to someone frozen in ice. For the first time in his life, Leonidas had been powerless to resist his desire.

But after tonight, when he told her the truth at his cocktail party—hell, from the moment she saw his *house*, when she obviously believed he lived in some grim studio apartment—he'd have no choice but to do without her.

Just thinking about it, Leonidas barely restrained himself all afternoon from biting the heads off his vice presidents and other employees when they dared ask him a question. But there was no point in blaming anyone else. It was his own fault.

Sitting in his private office, with its floor-to-ceiling windows with all of Manhattan at his feet, Leonidas gazed sightlessly over the city.

Was there any chance he could keep her?

Daisy Cassidy was in love with him. He'd seen her love in her beautiful face, shining in those pale green eyes, though she'd made some hopeless attempts to hide it. And she believed him to be some salesclerk in a Manhattan boutique. She loved him. Not for his billions. Not for his power. For himself.

If she could love some poverty-stricken salesclerk, couldn't she love Leonidas, too, flaws and all?

Maybe if he revealed why he'd been so angry about the Picasso, and the horrible secret of his childhood...

He shuddered. No. He could never tell anyone that. Or about his true parentage.

So how else could he convince her to stay?

Leonidas barely paid attention to a long, contentious board meeting, or the presentations of his brand presidents, discussing sales trends in luxury watches and jewelry in Asia and champagne and spirits in North America. Instead, he kept fantasizing about how, instead of losing Daisy with his confession tonight, he could manage to win her.

She would arrive at his cocktail party, he thought, and hopefully be dazzled by his famous guests, along with his fifty-million-dollar mansion. He would wait for just the right moment, then pull her away privately and explain. There would be awkwardness when she realized he'd been the one who'd arranged for his lawyer to press charges against her father. But Leonidas would make her understand. He'd seduce her with his words. With his touch. And with the lifestyle he could offer.

Daisy was living in the borrowed apartment of some middle-aged artist, an old friend of her father's. But if she came to live with Leonidas, as the cosseted girlfriend of a billionaire, she'd never have to worry about money again. He'd give her a life of luxury. She could quit her job at the diner and spend her days shopping or taking her friends to lunch, and her nights being worshipped by Leonidas in bed. They could travel around the world together, to London and Paris, Sydney, Rio and Tokyo, to his beach house in the Maldives, his ski chalet in Switzerland. He'd take her dancing, to parties, to the art shows and clubs and polo matches attended by the international jet set. He would shower her with gifts, expensive baubles beyond her imagination.

Surely all that could be enough to make her forgive and forget his part in her father's imprisonment? Surely such a life would be worth a little bit of constructive amnesia about her father? Who had been guilty, anyway!

Daisy had to forgive him, he thought suddenly. Why wouldn't she? Whatever Leonidas desired, he always possessed. Daisy Cassidy would be no different. He would pull out all the stops to win her. And though he'd never offer love or marriage, he knew he could make her happy. He'd treat her like the precious treasure she was, filling her days with joy, and her nights with fire.

Leonidas had never failed to seduce any woman he wanted. Tonight would be no different. He would make her forgive him. And forget her foolish loyalty to her dead father.

Tonight, Leonidas thought with determination, a sensual smile curving his lips. He would convince her tonight.

CHAPTER TWO

DAISY LOOKED UP at the five-story brownstone mansion with big eyes. There had to be some mistake.

"You're sure?" she asked the driver, bewildered.

The uniformed chauffeur hid a smile, dipping his head as he held open the passenger door. "Yes, miss."

Nervously, Daisy got out of the Rolls-Royce. She'd been astonished when the limo had picked her up in Brooklyn. Her neighborhood was prosperous, filled with a mix of artists and intellectuals, plumbers and stockbrokers. But a Rolls-Royce with a uniformed driver had made people stare. She'd been dismayed. The fancy French restaurant had been bad enough. How much had Leo spent renting this limo out? He shouldn't spend money he didn't have, just to impress her! She already thought he was perfect!

Although it was true she didn't know everything about him...

Standing on the sidewalk, she looked back up at the five-story mansion. This tree-lined lane in the West Village of Manhattan was filled with elegant houses only billionaires could afford. She craned her head doubtfully. "Is there a basement apartment?"

The chauffeur motioned toward the front steps. "The main entrance, miss. I believe the party has already started."

There was indeed a stream of limousines and town cars letting people out at the curb. An elderly couple went by Daisy, the wife in an elegant silk coat and matching dress, the husband in a suit.

She looked down at her own cocktail dress, which she'd borrowed from a friend. It was green satin, a little too tight and *way* too low in the bosom. Her cheap high heels, which she'd worn only once on a humiliating gallery night where she hadn't sold a single painting, squeezed her feet painfully.

She glanced behind her, longing to flee. But the driver had already gotten back into the Rolls-Royce and was driving away, to be immediately replaced by arriving vehicles, Italian and German sports cars attended by three valets waiting at the curb.

Daisy glanced toward the subway entrance at the far end of the lane, which ended in a busier street. She could make a run for it. Her puppy, who still didn't have a name, had been left in the care of the same friend, Estie, who'd been her pal in art school. Daisy could still go back home, cuddle the dog and eat popcorn and watch movies.

Except she couldn't. With a deep breath, she faced the brownstone mansion. She had to talk to Leo and tell him she was pregnant. Because she needed answers to her questions.

Would he help her raise the baby?

Would he marry her?

Could he love her?

Or would she face her future all on her own?

Swallowing hard, Daisy followed the elderly couple up the steps to the open door, where they were welcomed by a butler. As he looked over Daisy's ill-fitting cocktail dress and cheap shoes, the butler's eyebrows rose. "Your name, miss?"

"Daisy Cassidy." She held her breath, half expecting that, whatever the chauffeur had said, she'd been dropped at the wrong house and would be tossed out immediately.

Instead, the butler gave her a warm smile.

"We've been expecting you, Miss Cassidy. Welcome. Mrs. Berry," he glanced at a plump, white-haired woman nearby, "will take you inside."

"I'm Mr. Niarxos's housekeeper, Miss Cassidy," the older woman said kindly. "Will you please come this way?"

Bewildered, wondering who Mr. Niarxos was—

perhaps the butler?—Daisy followed the house-keeper through a lavish foyer. She gawked at the brief vision of a gold-painted ceiling above a crystal chandelier, high overhead, and a wide stone staircase that seemed straight out of *Downton Abbey*. They followed a steady crowd of glamorous guests through tall double doors into a ball-room.

Daisy's jaw dropped. A ballroom! In a house?

The ballroom was big enough to fit three hundred people, with a ceiling thirty feet high. The walls were gilded, and mirrors reflected the light of chandeliers that would have suited Versailles. Waiters wearing black tie walked through holding silver trays with champagne flutes on them. On the small stage, musicians played classical music.

Daisy felt like she'd just fallen through the floor to Wonderland. And there, across the ball-room—

Was that Leo in a tuxedo? Talking to the most famous movie star in the world?

"I'll tell him you're here, Miss Cassidy," Mrs. Berry said. "In the meantime, may I get you a drink?"

"What?" It took her a minute to understand the question. Yes. A stiff drink was an excellent idea. Then she remembered she was pregnant. "Uh...no. Thank you."

"Please wait here, Miss Cassidy." The white-haired woman departed with a respectful bow.

Across the crowds, she watched the house-keeper speak quietly to Leo on the other side of the ballroom. He turned, dark and powerful and devastatingly handsome. His eyes met Daisy's, and she felt a flash of fire.

Nervously, Daisy turned away to stare at a painting on the wall. It was a very nice framed print, a Jackson Pollock she didn't immediately recognize. Then her lips parted as she realized it probably wasn't a print. She was looking at a real Jackson Pollock. Just hanging in someone's home.

Although this didn't feel like a home. It felt like a royal palace. The castle of the king of New York...

"Daisy." Leo's voice was husky and low behind her. "I'm glad you came."

She whirled around. He was so close. Her knees trembled as her limbs went weak. "The puppy is fine," she blurted out. "If you were worried."

"Oh. Good." His expression didn't change. He towered over her, powerful and broad shouldered, the focus of all the glamorous guests sipping cocktails in the ballroom. And no wonder. Daisy's gaze traced unwillingly from his hard jawline, now smoothly shaved, to the sharp cheekbones and his cruel, sensual mouth. How could she tell him she'd fallen in love with him? How could she tell him she was pregnant?

"Thank you for inviting me." She bit her

lip, looking around at the glittering ballroom. "Whose house is this really?"

His black eyes burned through her. "It's mine."

She laughed. Then saw he was serious. "But how can it be?" she stammered. Her forehead furrowed. "Are you a member of the staff here?"

"No. I work for Liontari."

"Is that a store?"

"It's a company. We own luxury brands around the world."

"Oh." She felt relieved. So he *did* work for a shop. "Your employer owns this mansion? They're the ones throwing the party?"

"I told you, Daisy. The house is mine."

"But how?" Did being a salesclerk pay better than she could possibly imagine? Was he the best salesman in the world?

Leo looked down at her, then sighed.

"I never told you my full name," he said slowly. "Leonidas Gianakos… Niarxos."

He stared down at her, waiting. A faint warning bell rang at the back of her head. She couldn't quite remember where she'd heard it before. From the butler at the front door? Or before that? She repeated, "Niarxos?"

"Yes." And still he waited, watching her. As if he expected some reaction.

"Oh." Feeling awkward, she said, "So who is this fundraiser for?"

Looking relieved, he named a politician she'd

vaguely heard of. She looked around the gilded ballroom. This party was very fancy, that was for sure. She saw people she recognized. Actors. Entrepreneurs. And even—she sucked in her breath. A world-famous artist, which impressed her most of all.

What was Daisy even doing here, with all these chic, glamorous people, people she should properly only read about in magazines or social media, or see on the big screen?

"How—" she began, then her throat dried up.

Across the ballroom, she saw someone else she recognized. Someone she'd glared at every day for a month. Someone she'd never, ever forget. A gray-haired villain in a suit.

Edgar Ross.

The lawyer who'd called the police on her father. The last time she'd seen him, he'd been sitting behind the prosecutor in the courtroom. A ruthless lawyer who worked for an even more ruthless boss, some foreign-born billionaire.

"Daisy?" Leo looked down at her, his handsome face concerned. "What is it?"

"It's… It's… What is he—"

At that moment, Edgar Ross himself came over to them, with a pretty middle-aged blonde on his arm. "Good evening, Mr. Niarxos."

Daisy's lips parted as Leo greeted the man with a warm handshake. "Good evening." He gave the blonde a polite peck on the cheek. "Mrs. Ross."

"It's a great party. Thanks for inviting us." Edgar Ross smiled vaguely at Daisy, as if he were trying to place her.

She stared back coldly, shaking with the effort it took not to slap him, wishing she'd taken a glass of champagne after all, so she could throw it in his face. Including the glass.

"Admiring your most recent acquisition?" Ross asked Leo. For a moment, Daisy thought he meant *her*. Then she realized he was referring to the painting on the wall.

He shrugged. "It's an investment."

"Of course," Ross said, smiling. "It will just have to hold you, until we can find that Picasso, eh?"

The Picasso.

It all clicked horrifyingly into place. Daisy suddenly couldn't breathe.

Edgar Ross.

The Picasso.

The wealthy billionaire reported to be behind it all. The Greek billionaire.

Leonidas Niarxos.

In the background, the orchestra continued to play, and throughout the ballroom, people continued to talk and laugh. As if the world hadn't just collapsed.

Daisy slowly turned with wide, stricken eyes.

"Leo," she choked out, feeling like she was about to faint. Feeling like she was about to die.

He looked down at her, then his expression changed. "No," he said in a low voice. "Daisy, wait."

But she was already backing away. Her knees were shaking. The high heel of her shoe twisted, and she barely caught herself from falling.

No. The truth was she hadn't caught herself. She'd fallen in love with Leo, her first and only lover. He'd taken her virginity. He was the father of her unborn baby.

But Leo didn't exist.

He was actually *Leonidas Niarxos*. Edgar Ross's boss. The Greek billionaire behind everything. The real reason the prosecutor and the judge had thrown the book at her father, penalizing him to the fullest extent of the law, when he should have just been fined in civil court—or better yet, found innocent. But no. With his money and power, Leonidas Niarxos had been determined to get his pound of flesh. The spoiled billionaire, who already owned million-dollar paintings and palaces, hadn't gotten the toy he wanted, so he'd destroyed her father's life.

A year ago, when her father had been convicted of forgery, Daisy had been heartbroken, because she'd known he was innocent. Her father was a good man. The best. He never would have broken the law. She'd been shocked and sickened that somehow, in a miscarriage of justice, he'd still been found guilty. Then, six months ago,

Patrick had died of a stroke, alone and scared, in a prison surrounded by strangers.

Daisy had vowed that if she ever had the chance, she would take her revenge. She, who'd never wanted to hurt anyone, who always tried to see the best in everyone, wanted *vengeance*.

But she'd naively given Leo everything. Her smiles. Her kisses. Her body. Her love. She was even carrying his baby, deep inside her.

Daisy stared up at Leo's heartbreakingly handsome face. The face she'd loved. So much.

No. He wasn't Leo. She could never think of him as Leo again.

He was Leonidas Niarxos. The man who'd killed her father.

"Oh, my God." Edgar Ross stared at Daisy, his eyes wide. "You're Cassidy's daughter. I didn't recognize you in that dress. What are you doing here?"

Yes, what? The ballroom, with its gilded glitter, started to swim in front of her eyes.

Daisy's breaths came in short wheezing gasps, constricted as her chest was by the too-tight cocktail dress. With every breath, her breasts pushed higher against the low neckline. She felt like she was going to pass out.

She had to get out of there.

But as she turned away, Leonidas grabbed her wrist.

"No!" she yelled, and wrenched her arm away.

Everyone turned to stare at them in shock, and the music stopped.

For a moment, he just looked down at her, his handsome face hard. He didn't try to touch her again.

"We need to talk," he said through gritted teeth.

"What could you possibly have to say to me?" she choked out, hatred rising through her, filling every inch of her hollow heart. She gave a low, brittle laugh. "Did you enjoy your little joke? Seducing me? Laughing at me?"

"Daisy…"

"You took *everything*!" Her voice was a rasp. She felt used. And so fragile that a single breeze might scatter her to the wind. "How could you have lied to me? Pretending to love me—"

"I didn't lie—"

"You lied," she said flatly.

"I never claimed to love you."

His dark eyes glittered as they stared at each other.

All around them, the glamorous people were frankly staring, tilting their heads slightly to hear. As if Daisy hadn't been humiliated enough last year by the New York press gleefully calling her beloved, innocent father names like *con artist* and *fraud*, and even worse, calling him too stupid to properly commit a crime.

But she was the one who was stupid. All along,

she'd known Leo was hiding things from her. She'd ignored her fears and convinced herself he was perfect. She'd trusted her heart.

Her stupid, stupid heart.

Her shoulders sagged, and her eyes stung. She blinked fast, wiping her eyes savagely.

"Daisy." Leonidas's voice was a low growl. "Just give me a moment. Alone. Let me explain."

She was trembling, her teeth chattering almost loud enough to hear. There was nothing he could possibly say that would take away her sense of betrayal. She should slap his face and leave, and never look him in the face again.

But their baby.

Her joints hurt with heartbreak, pain rushing through her veins, pounding a toxic rhythm. Her heart shut down, and she went numb. Whatever he'd done, he was still her baby's father. She had to tell him.

"I'll give you one minute," she choked out.

Leonidas gestured toward the ballroom's double doors. She followed him out of the glittering, glamorous ballroom, away from the curious crowd, into the deserted foyer of the New York mansion. Wordlessly, she followed him up the wide stone staircase, to the dark quiet of the hallway upstairs.

She felt like a ghost of the girl she'd been. As they climbed the staircase, she glanced up at his dark shadow, and felt sick inside.

Discovering she was pregnant earlier that day, she'd felt so alone, so scared. Her first thought had been that she couldn't raise a child without him. But now, Daisy suddenly realized there was something even more terrifying than raising a baby alone.

Doing it with your worst enemy.

As Leonidas led Daisy past the security guards in the foyer, up the wide stone staircase of his New York mansion, his heart was beating oddly fast.

He glanced back at her.

Daisy looked so beautiful in the emerald green cocktail dress, with high heels showing off her slender legs. Her long honey-brown hair brushed against her shoulders, over the spaghetti straps, past the low-cut neckline which revealed full breasts, plumped up by the tight satin. Against his will, his eyes lingered there. Had her breasts always been so big? Just watching the sensuous way she moved her hand along the stone bannister, he imagined being the one she touched, and he stirred in spite of himself.

But her eyes were downcast, her dark lashes trembling angrily against her pale cheeks.

Leonidas wondered what she was thinking. It was strange. He'd never cared before about what his lovers might be thinking. And with Daisy, he'd always been able to read her feelings on her face.

Until now.

She glanced up at him, her lovely face carefully blank. She looked back down as they climbed the sweeping staircase.

This was not how Leonidas had hoped this evening would go.

Thinking about it at the office, he'd pictured Daisy being dazzled by his mansion, by the glitter and prestige of his guests, by his wealth and power. He'd convinced himself that she would be in a receptive frame of mind to learn the truth. That Daisy would be shocked, dismayed, even, to learn his identity, but she would swiftly forgive him. Because he was so obviously right.

Daisy loved her father. But she had to see that Patrick Cassidy had been a criminal, protecting his accomplice to the end, refusing to say who'd painted the fake Picasso. What else could Leonidas have done but have his lawyer press charges? Should he have paid millions for a painting he knew was fake, or allowed someone else to potentially be defrauded? He'd done the right thing.

Obviously Daisy didn't see it that way. He had to help her see it from his perspective. Setting his jaw, he led her down the dark, empty upstairs hallway and pushed open the second door, switching on the bedroom light.

She stopped in the doorway, glaring at him.

He felt irritated at her accusatory gaze. Did she really think he'd brought her into his bedroom to seduce her? That he intended to simply toss her on the bed and cover her with kisses until the past was forgiven and forgotten?

If only!

Leonidas forced himself to take a deep breath. He kept his voice calm and reassuring, just the way Daisy had spoken when she'd held that abandoned puppy in the alley.

"I'm just bringing you in here to talk," he said soothingly. "Where no one else can hear us."

She flashed him another glance he couldn't read, but came into the bedroom. He closed the door softly behind her.

His bedroom was Spartan, starkly decorated with a king-sized bed, walk-in closet and a lot of open space. Through a large window, he could see the orange and red leaves of the trees on the quiet lane outside, darkening in the twilight.

Standing near the closed door, Daisy wrapped her arms around herself as if for protection, and said in a low voice, "Did you know who I was? The day we met?"

He could not lie to her. "Yes."

She lifted pale green eyes, swimming with tears. "Why did you seduce me? For a laugh? For revenge?"

"No, Daisy, no—" He tried to move toward her, wanting to take her in his arms, to offer comfort. But she moved violently back before he could touch her. He froze, dropping his hands. "I saw a drawing of the trial, when your father's verdict was read. It made me feel sorry for you."

The emotion in her face changed to anger. "*Sorry* for me?"

That hadn't come out right. "I heard your father died in prison, and I came looking for you because…because I wanted to make sure you were all right. And perhaps give you some money."

"Money?" Her expression hardened. "Do you really think that could compensate me for my father's death? Some… some *payoff*?"

"That was never my intention, it—" Leonidas cut himself off, gritting his teeth. He forced his voice to remain calm. "You never deserved to suffer. *You* were innocent."

"So was my father!"

Against his best intentions, his own anger rose. "You cannot be so blind as to think that your father was innocent. Of course he wasn't. He tried to sell a forgery."

"Then he foolishly trusted the wrong person. Someone must have tricked him and convinced him the painting was real. He never would have tried to sell it otherwise! He was a good man! Perfect!"

"Are you kidding? Your father was selling forgeries for years."

"No one else ever accused him—"

"Because either they were too embarrassed, or

they didn't realize the paintings were fakes. Your father knew he wasn't selling a real Picasso."

"How would he know that? No one has seen the painting for decades. How did that lawyer lackey of yours even know it wasn't real?"

Leonidas had a flash of memory from twenty years before. His misery as a boy at his parents' strange neglect and hatred. The shock of his mother's final abandonment. His heartbroken fury, as a boy of fourteen. He could still feel the cold steel in his hand. The canvas ripping beneath his blade in the violent joy of destruction, of finally giving in to his rage—

Looking away, Leonidas said tightly, "I was the one who knew it was a fake. From the moment I saw it in Ross's office."

"You." Daisy glared at him in the cold silence of his bedroom, across the enormous bed, which he'd so recently dreamed of sharing with her. "Why couldn't you just let it go? What's one Picasso to you, more or less?"

Leonidas's shoulders tightened. He didn't want to think about what it meant to him. Or why he'd been looking for it so desperately for two decades.

"So I should have just let your father get away with his deceit?" he said coldly. "Allowed him to continue passing off fake paintings?"

"My father was innocent!" Her expression was fierce. "He looked into my eyes and *swore* it!"

"Because he couldn't bear for you to know the truth. He loved you too much."

Anguish shone in her beautiful face. Then her expression crumpled.

"And I loved him," she said brokenly. She wiped her eyes. "But you're wrong. He never would have lied to me. He had no reason—"

"You would have forgiven him?"

"Yes."

"Because you loved him." Leonidas took a deep breath and looked into her eyes. "So forgive me," he whispered.

She sucked in her breath. "What?"

"You're in love with me, Daisy. We both know that."

Her lush pink lips parted. She seemed to tremble. "What...how—"

"I've seen it on your face. Heard it in your voice. You're in love—" He took a step toward her, but she put her hand up, warding him off.

"I loved a man who doesn't exist." She looked up, her green eyes glittering. "Not you. I could never love you."

Her words stabbed him like a physical attack. He heard echoes of his mother's harsh voice, long ago.

Stop bothering me. I'm sick of your whimpering. Leave me alone.

Leonidas had spent three decades distancing himself from that five-year-old boy, becoming rich and powerful and strong, to make sure he'd never feel like that again. And now this.

Senseless, overwhelming rage filled him.

"You could never love a man like me?" He lifted his chin. "But you're full of love for a liar like your father?"

"Don't you call him that. *You're* the liar! Don't you dare even *speak* of him—"

"He was a criminal, Daisy. And you're a fool," he said harshly.

"You're right. I am." Her lovely face was pale, her clenched hands shaking at her sides. "But you're a monster. You took everything. My father. My home. My self-respect. My virginity..."

"Your father made his own bed." He looked down at her coldly. "So did you."

Her lips parted in a gasp.

"I never took anything that wasn't willingly— *enthusiastically*—given to me," he continued ruthlessly.

"I hate myself for ever letting you touch me," she whispered. Her tearful eyes lifted to his. "I wish I could hurt you like you've hurt me."

Leonidas barked a humorless laugh. "You can't."

New rage filled her beautiful face. "Why? Because you think I'm so powerless? So meaningless?"

"No." He wasn't being rude. If Daisy knew

about the pain of his childhood, he suspected it would satisfy even her current vengeful mood.

But she couldn't know. Leonidas intended to keep those memories buried until the day he died, buried deep in the graveyard that existed beneath his ribs, in place of a heart.

"I hate you," she choked out. "You don't deserve—"

"What?" he said, when she didn't finish. "What don't I deserve?"

She turned her head away. "You don't deserve another moment of my time."

Her voice was low and certain, and it filled him with despair. How had he ever thought he could win her?

Leonidas saw now that he'd never make her see his side. She hated him, just as he'd always known she would, the moment she learned his name.

It was over.

"If you think I'm such a monster," he said hoarsely, "what are you still doing here? Why don't you go?"

She stared at him, her arms wrapped around her belly. For a moment, she seemed frozen in indecision. Then—

"You're right," she said finally. She crossed the bedroom and opened the door. He briefly smelled her perfume, the scent of sunshine and roses. As she passed him, he could almost feel the warmth from her skin, from her curves barely contained beneath the tight green dress. "I never should have come up here." She gave him one last look. "As far as I'm concerned, the man I loved is dead."

Daisy walked out of his bedroom without another glance, disappearing into the shadows of the hall. And she left Leonidas, alone in his mansion, feeling like a monster, surrounded by rich and powerful friends, in a world that was even more dark and bleak than it had been before he'd met her.

CHAPTER THREE

Five months later

IT WAS EARLY MARCH, but in New York, there was no whisper of warmth, not yet. It was gray and cold, and the sidewalks were edged with dirty snow from a storm a few days before. Even the trees had not yet started to bud. The weather still felt miserably like winter.

But for Daisy, spring had already begun.

She took a deep breath, hugging herself as she stepped out of the obstetrician's office. At six months' pregnant, her belly had grown so big she was barely able to zip up her long black puffy coat. She'd had to get new clothes from thrift shops and friends with discarded maternity outfits; aside from her swelling belly, she'd put on a good amount of pregnancy weight.

After a six-hour morning shift at the diner, Daisy had already been exhausted before she'd skipped lunch to go straight to a doctor's appointment. But the medical office had been running late, and she'd sat in the waiting room for an hour. Now, as she finally left, her stomach was growling, and she thought with pity of her dog at home, waiting for her meal, too.

She quickened her step, her breath a white cloud in cold air that was threatening rain. She couldn't stop smiling.

Her checkup had gone perfectly. Her baby was doing well, her pregnancy was on track, and after the morning sickness misery of her first trimester, and the uncertainty of her second, now she was in her final trimester. She finally felt like she knew what she was doing. She felt...*hope*.

It was funny, she thought, as she hurried down the crowded Brooklyn sidewalk, vibrant with colorful shops. Her past was filled with tragedy that she once would have thought she could not survive: her mother's illness and death when Daisy was seven, her own failure at becoming an artist, her father's accusation and trial followed by his sudden death, falling in love with Leo and accidentally getting pregnant then finding out he was actually Leonidas Niarxos.

She had decided to raise her baby alone, rather than with a man who didn't deserve to be her child's father, but it was strange now to remember how, five months ago, she'd been so sure she wasn't strong or brave enough to do it alone. But the fight with Leonidas at his cocktail party had made it clear she had no other choice.

And she'd made it through. She was stronger and wiser. She'd never again be so stupidly innocent, giving her heart to someone she barely knew. She'd never be that young again.

Becoming an adult—a *mother*—meant making responsible choices. She'd given up childish dreams of romance, and someday becoming an artist. Her baby was all that mattered. Daisy put a hand on her belly over her black puffy coat. She'd found out a few months earlier she was having a little girl.

Daisy's friends in Brooklyn had rallied around her. Claudia Vogler, her boss at the diner, had given her extra hours so Daisy could save money. She'd forgiven all of Daisy's missed shifts due to morning sickness, and, when Daisy started having trouble being on her feet all day, Claudia had even created a new job for her—to sit by the cash register at the diner and ring out customers. Since most customers just paid their server directly with a credit card, Daisy mostly just greeted them as they came, and said goodbye as they left.

And she was still living in Franck's apartment, rent free. The middle-aged artist had returned to New York a week after her breakup with Leonidas. He'd been shocked, walking into his apartment, expensive suitcase in hand, to discover a puppy living in his home, which was full of easily breakable sculptures and expensive modern art on the walls.

She'd named her puppy Sunny, to remind herself, even in the depths of her worry, to focus on the brightness all around her. But Sunny was an excitable puppy, and she'd already managed to pee on his rug and chew Franck's slippers.

"I'm so sorry," Daisy had choked out, confessing her puppy's sins. She'd half expected him to throw both her and the dog out.

But to her surprise, Franck had been kind. He'd allowed her to keep the dog and told her she could stay at his apartment as long as she liked, since he was leaving anyway, to snowbird at his house in Los Angeles. That had been in October.

She'd fallen to her lowest point in early January, shivering in the depths of a gray winter despair, she'd felt scared and alone.

Franck, returning to New York on a two-day business trip, had discovered Daisy sitting on the fireside rug, crying into Sunny's fur. When she'd looked up, the gray-haired man had seemed like a surrogate for the father she missed so much, and she'd tearfully told him about her unexpected pregnancy, and that the baby's father was no longer in the picture.

He'd been shocked. After vaguely comforting her, he'd left for his studio. He'd returned late, sleeping in his bedroom down the hall.

Then, the next morning at the breakfast table, right before his return flight to Los Angeles, Franck had abruptly offered to marry her.

Overwhelmed, Daisy had stammered, "You're so kind, Franck, but... I have no intention of marrying anyone."

It was true. In addition to the fact that he was so much older, and had obviously asked her out of pity, Daisy had no desire to marry anyone. Getting her heart broken once was enough for a lifetime.

Franck had seemed strangely disappointed at her refusal. "You're in shock. You'll change your mind," he'd said. And no amount of protesting on her part had made him think differently. "But whether you marry me or not, you're welcome to stay here," he'd added softly, looking down at her. "Stay as long as you want. Stay forever."

It had all been a little awkward. She'd been relieved when he'd left for Los Angeles.

But hearing Franck describe how lovely and warm it was in California had given her an idea. She'd had a sudden memory of her father, two years before.

Daisy had been crying after her first gallery show, heartbroken over her failure to sell a single painting, when her father had said, "We could start over. Move to Santa Barbara, where I was born. It's a beautiful place, warm and bright. We could buy a little cottage by the sea, with a garden full of flowers."

"Leave New York?" Wiping her eyes in surprise, Daisy had looked at him. "What about your gallery, Dad?"

"Maybe I'd like a change, too. Just one more deal to close, and then…we'll see."

Shortly after that, Patrick had been arrested, and there had been no more talk of fresh starts.

But the memory suddenly haunted Daisy. Pregnant and alone, she found herself yearning for her parents' love more than ever. For comfort, for sunshine and warmth, for flowers and the sea.

Her mother had once been a nurse, before she'd gotten sick. Daisy liked helping people, and she knew her income as a waitress would not be enough to support a child, at least not in Brooklyn. She needed grown-up things, like financial security and insurance benefits. Why not?

Holding her breath, Daisy had applied to a small nursing school in Santa Barbara.

Miraculously, she'd been accepted, and with a scholarship, too. She would start school in the fall, when her baby was three months old.

Soon after, her morning sickness had disappeared. She'd managed to save some money, and she had a plan for her future.

But now, Franck was due to return to New York next week for good. Daisy couldn't imagine sharing his apartment with him. She needed to move out.

Where else could she live? None of her friends had extra space, and she couldn't afford to rent her own apartment, not when she was saving every penny for baby expenses and moving expenses. It was a problem.

If she'd had enough money, she would have left for California immediately. In New York City, she was scared of accidentally running into Leonidas. If he ever learned she was pregnant, he might try to take custody of their baby. She was desperate to be free of him. Desperate for a clean break.

But she had a job here, friends here, and—as uncomfortable as it might make her—at least at Franck's, she had a roof over her head. She just had to hold on until summer. Her baby was due in early June. By the end of August, she'd have money to get a deposit on a new apartment, and the two of them could start a new life in California.

Until then, she just had to cross her fingers and pray Leonidas wouldn't come looking for her.

He won't. It will all work out, Daisy told herself, as she had so many times over the last few months. *I'll be fine.*

The difference was, she'd finally started to believe it.

In the distance, dark clouds were threatening rain, and she could see her breath in the cold air. Quickening her pace, Daisy started humming softly as she hurried home. She'd heard that a baby, even in the womb, could hear her mother's voice, so she'd started talking and singing to her at all hours. As she sang aloud, some tourists looked at her with alarm. Daisy giggled. Just another crazy New Yorker, walking down the street and singing to herself!

Reaching her co-op building, she greeted the doorman with a smile. "Hey, Walter."

"Good afternoon, Miss Cassidy. How's that baby?" he asked sweetly, as he always did.

"Wonderful," she replied, and took the elevator to the top floor.

As she came through the door, her dog, Sunny, still a puppy at heart in spite of having grown so big, bounded up with a happy bark, tail waving her body frantically. She acted as if Daisy had been gone for months, rather than hours. With a laugh, Daisy petted her lavishly, then went to the kitchen to put food in her dog dish.

She didn't bother to take off her coat. She knew how this would go. As expected, Sunny gulped down her food, then immediately leaped back to the door with a happy bark. Daisy sighed a little to herself. Sunny did love her walks. Even when it was cold and threatening rain.

Grabbing the leash, Daisy attached it to the dog's collar and left the apartment.

Once outside, she took a deep breath of the cold, damp air. It was late afternoon as she took the dog for their usual walk along the river path. By the time they returned forty minutes later, the drizzle was threatening to deepen into rain, and the sun was falling in the west, streaking the fiery sky red and orange, silhouetting the sharp Manhattan skyline across the East River. As busy as she'd been, she'd forgotten to eat that day, and she was starving. Seeing her co-op building ahead, Daisy hurried her pace, fantasizing about what she'd have for dinner.

Then she saw the black Rolls-Royce parked in front of the building. A chill went down her spine as a towering, dark-haired figure got out of the limo.

She stopped cold, causing a surprised yelp from Sunny. She wanted to turn and run—a ridiculous idea, when she knew Leonidas Niarxos could easily run her down, with his powerful body and long legs.

Their eyes met, and he came forward grimly.

She couldn't move, staring at his darkly powerful form, with the backdrop view of the majestic bridge and red sunset.

Please, she thought as he approached. Let her black puffy coat be enough to hide her pregnancy. Please, please.

But her hope was crushed with his very first words.

"So it's true?" Leonidas's voice was dangerously low, his black eyes gleaming like white-hot coal in the twilight. He looked down at her belly, bulging out beneath the long black puffy coat. "You're pregnant?"

Instinctively, she wrapped her hands over her baby bump. How had he heard? She trembled all over. "What are you doing here?"

"Are you, Daisy?"

She could hardly deny it. "Yes."

His burning gaze met hers. "Is the baby mine?"

She swallowed hard, wanting more than anything to lie.

But she couldn't. Even though Leonidas had lied to her about his identity, and lied about Daisy's father, she couldn't fall to his level. She couldn't lie to his face. Not even for her child.

What kind of mother would she be, if she practiced the same deceit as Leonidas Niarxos? She felt somehow, even in the womb, that her baby was listening. And she had to prove herself worthy. She, at least, was a good person. *Unlike him.*

"Am I the father, Daisy?" he pressed.

Stiffening, Daisy lifted her chin defiantly. "Only biologically."

"Only?" Leonidas's eyes went wide, then narrowed. Setting his jaw, he walked slowly around her, as if searching for weaknesses. He ignored her dog, who traitorously wagged her tail at him. "Why didn't you tell me?"

"Why would I?"

"Because it's the decent thing to do?"

She glared at him. "You don't deserve to be her father."

Leonidas stopped, as if he'd been punched in

the gut. Then he said evenly, "You are legally entitled to child support."

She tossed her head. "I don't want it."

"You'd really let your pride override the best interests of the child?"

"Pride!" she breathed. "Is that what you think?"

"What else could it be? You want to hurt me. You don't care that it also injures our baby in the process."

It was strange, Daisy thought, that even after all this time, he could still find new ways to hurt her.

It didn't help that Leonidas was even more devastatingly handsome than she remembered, standing in the twilight dressed in black from head to toe, in his dark suit covered by a long dark coat. His clothing was sleek, but his black hair was rumpled, and his sharp jawline was edged with five o'clock shadow. Everything about him seemed dark in this moment.

"This isn't about you," she ground out. "It's about her. She doesn't need a father like you—a liar with no soul!"

For a moment, they glared at each other as they stood on the empty pathway along the East River, with the brilliant backdrop of Manhattan's skyline against the red sunset. Her harsh words hung between them like toxic mist.

"You only hate me because I told the truth

about your father." His voice was low. "But I am not the one you should hate. I never lied to you."

"How can you say that?" She was outraged. "From the day we met, when you told me your name—"

"I didn't tell you my full name. But that was only because I liked talking to you and didn't want it to end." His deep voice was quiet. "I never lied. I never tried to sell a forgery. I am not the criminal."

She caught her breath, and for a moment she felt dizzy, wondering if he could be telling the truth. Could her father have been guilty? Had he known the Picasso was a forgery when he'd tried to sell it?

I didn't do it, baby. I swear it on my life. On my love for you.

Daisy remembered the tremble in her father's voice, the emotion gleaming in his eyes the night of his arrest. All throughout his trial and subsequent imprisonment, he'd maintained his innocence, saying he'd been duped just like his wealthy customers. But he'd refused to say who had duped him.

Who was she going to believe—the perfect father who'd raised her and loved her, caring for her as a single parent after her mother died, or the selfish billionaire who'd had him dragged into court, who'd taken Daisy's virginity and left her pregnant and alone?

"Don't you dare call my father a criminal!"

"He was convicted. He went to prison."

"Where he died—thanks to you!" Her voice was a rasp. "You ruined his life out of spite, over a painting that meant nothing—"

"That painting means more than—"

"You ruined my life on a selfish whim." Daisy's voice rose. "Why would I want you near my baby, so you could wreck her life as well? Just go away, and leave us alone!"

Leonidas stared at her in shock. He'd never imagined that he'd become a father. And he'd never imagined that his baby's mother could hate him so much.

The soft drizzle had turned to sleet, falling from the darkening sky. Nearby, he could almost hear the rush of the East River, the muffled roar of traffic from the looming bridge.

Just go away, and leave us alone.

He heard the echo of his mother's voice when he was five years old.

Stop bothering me. I'm sick of your whimpering. Leave me alone.

Since their breakup last October, through a gray fall and grayer winter, Leonidas had tried to keep thoughts of Daisy at bay. Yes, she was beautiful. But so what? The world was full of beautiful women. Yes, she was clever. Diabolically so, since she'd lured him so easily into wanting her, into believing she was different from the rest. Into believing her love could somehow save his soul and make him a better man.

Ridiculous. It humiliated him to remember. He'd acted like a fool, believing their connection had been based on anything more than sexual desire.

He couldn't let down his guard. He couldn't let himself depend on anyone's love.

Daisy Cassidy had been the most exhilarating lover he'd ever had, but she was also the most dangerous. He'd needed to get her out of his life. Out from beneath his skin.

So the day after their argument, he'd left New York, vowing to forget her. And he had.

By day.

But night was a different matter. His body could not forget. Against his will, all these months later, he still dreamed of her, erotic dreams of a sensual virgin, luring him inexorably to his destruction. In the dream, he gave her everything— not just his body, not just his fortune, he gave her his heart. Then she always took it in her grasp and crushed it to dripping blood and burned ash.

Two days before, he'd woken after one particularly agonizing dream at his luxury apartment on the Boulevard Saint-Germain in Paris, gasping and filled with despair.

Ever since their affair had ended, his days had been gray. He barely cared about the billion-dollar conglomerate which had once been his passion. Even his formerly docile board was starting to whisper that perhaps he should step down as CEO.

Leonidas could hardly blame them. He'd lost his appetite for business. He'd lost his edge. The truth was, he just didn't give a damn anymore. How long would he be tormented by these dreams of her—dreams that could never again be real?

Then he'd suddenly gotten angry.

He realized he hadn't visited his company's headquarters back in New York once since that disastrous cocktail party. Daisy had driven him out of the city. He'd left his ex-girlfriend in victorious possession of the entire continent. But even on the other side of the world, she destroyed his peace.

No longer.

Grimly, he'd called his chief of security at the New York office. "Find out about Daisy Cassidy. I want to know what she's doing."

Then he'd called his pilot to arrange the flight back to New York. He was done running from her. He'd done nothing wrong. *Nothing.* Maybe, once he was back amid the hum and energy of his company's headquarters, he'd regain some of his old passion for the luxury business.

But he didn't relish the thought of Daisy ambushing him at some Manhattan event, or seeing her on another man's arm. He hoped his chief of security would tell him she'd moved to Miami—or better yet, Siberia. Either way, Leonidas wanted to be prepared.

But he'd had no defense against what his security chief had told him.

Daisy Cassidy was six months pregnant, according to her friends. And refusing to say who the father might be.

But Leonidas knew. Daisy had been a virgin their first night, and she'd been faithful for the month of their affair—he had no doubt of that.

The baby had to be his.

Leonidas had felt restless, jittery, on the flight back to New York yesterday, wondering if she'd already known she was pregnant the night she'd walked out on him. Back at his West Village mansion, he'd collapsed, and slept like the dead. But at least he hadn't been tormented by dreams.

Waking up late, he'd gone to the office, but had lasted only two hours before he'd called his driver to take him across the river. He'd waited outside the Brooklyn co-op where Daisy lived, tension building inside him as he tried to decide whether to go inside. Once he confirmed her pregnancy, there would be no going back.

Then he saw her, walking her dog on the street.

Leonidas hadn't been able to tear his eyes away. Daisy was more beautiful than ever, her green eyes shining, her face radiant, and her body lush with pregnancy. She'd gained some weight, and her fuller curves suited her, making her even more impossibly desirable.

Why hadn't she told him she was pregnant? Did she really hate him so much that she wouldn't even accept his financial support for their child? It seemed incredibly reckless and wrong. She could have been pampered in her pregnancy. Instead, by all accounts she was still working on her feet as a waitress, and living in another man's apartment. The same apartment where she and Leonidas had conceived this child. No wonder he felt so off-kilter and dizzy.

Then she'd said it.

Just go away, and leave us alone.

Leonidas stared at her, still shocked that the tenderhearted girl who'd once claimed to love him could say anything so cruel. His whole body felt tight, his heart rate increasing as his hands clenched at his sides.

His voice was hoarse as he said, "You really believe I'm such a monster that you need to hide your pregnancy from me? You won't even let me support my own child?"

Daisy's expression filled with shadow in the twilight, as if even she realized she'd gone too far.

"We don't need you," she said finally, and turning, she hurried away, almost running with her dog following behind, disappearing into the apartment building.

You little monster. His mother's enraged voice, when he was fourteen. *I wish you'd never been born!*

For a moment, the image of the bleak bridge and water swam before Leonidas's eyes, malevolent and dark against the red twilight. His heart hammered in his throat, his body tense.

Those had been his mother's final words, the last time Leonidas saw her. He'd been fourteen, and had just come from the funeral of the man he'd always believed was his father, when his mother had told him the truth, and that she never intended to see Leonidas again. Heartsick, he'd hacked into her precious masterpiece with a pair of scissors. Ripping the broken Picasso from his hands, his mother had left him with those final words.

She'd died in the Turkish earthquake a week later, and the Picasso had disappeared. That day, Leonidas had lost his only blood relative in the world.

Until now.

Leonidas looked up at the co-op building, with its big windows overlooking the river. His eyes narrowed dangerously.

Daisy had kept her pregnancy a secret, because she didn't want him to be a father to their baby.

Why would I want you near my baby, so you could wreck her life as well?

Her life. Leonidas suddenly realized the import of Daisy's words. They were having a baby girl.

And whether Daisy liked it or not, Leonidas was going to be a father. He would soon have a daughter who'd need him to protect and provide for her. This baby was his family.

His only family.

Gripping his hands at his sides, Leonidas went toward the building. He gave a sharp shake of his head to his driver, waiting with the Rolls-Royce at the curb, and went forward alone into the apartment building. He opened the door, going into the contemporary glass-and-steel lobby, with modern, sparse furniture. He headed straight for the elevator, until he found his way blocked.

"Can I help you, sir?" the doorman demanded.

"Daisy Cassidy," he barked in reply. "I know the apartment number."

"You must wait," the man replied. Going to the reception desk, the man picked up his phone. "Your name, sir?"

"Leonidas Niarxos."

The doorman spoke quietly into the phone, then looked up. "I'm sorry, Miss Cassidy says she has nothing to say to you. She asks you to leave the building immediately."

A curse went through his mind. "Tell her she can talk to me now or talk to an army of lawyers in an hour."

The doorman raised his eyebrows, then again spoke quietly. With a sigh, he hung up the phone. "She says to go up, Mr. Niarxos."

"Yes," he bit out. He stalked to the elevator, feeling the doorman's silently accusing eyes on his back. But Leonidas didn't give a damn. His fury sustained him as he pushed the elevator button for the fifth floor.

He straightened, his jaw tight. He was no longer a helpless five-year-old. No longer a heartsick fourteen-year-old. He was a man now. A man with power and wealth. A man who could take what he wanted.

And he wasn't going to let Daisy steal his child away.

The elevator gave a cheerful ding as the door slid open. He grimly stalked down the hall to apartment 502. Lifting his hand, he gave a single hard knock.

The door opened, and he saw Daisy's furious, tear-stained face.

In spite of everything, his heart twisted at the sight. Her pale green eyes, fringed with thick black lashes, were luminous against her skin, with a few adorable freckles scattered across her nose. Her lips were pink and full, as she chewed on her lower lip, as if trying to bite back angry words.

Her body, in the fullness of pregnancy, was lush and feminine. She'd taken off her long puffy coat, and was dressed simply, in a long-sleeved white shirt over black leggings. But she was somehow even more alluring to him than the night of the cocktail party, when she'd been wearing that low-cut green dress, with her breasts overflowing. He'd thought the dress was simply tight, but now he realized her breasts had already been swollen by pregnancy. Pregnant. With his baby.

A baby she was trying to keep from Leonidas, who was here and ready to take responsibility. Who wanted to be a father!

Interesting. He blinked. He hadn't realized it until now. He'd always thought he had no interest in fatherhood, no interest in settling down. What did he know about being a good parent?

But now he wanted it more than anything.

Daisy tossed her head with an angry, shuddering breath. "How dare you threaten me with lawyers?"

"How dare you try to steal my child?" he retorted, pushing into the apartment without touching her.

It was the first time he'd been back here since their days as lovers. The apartment looked just as he remembered, modern and new, with a gas fireplace and an extraordinary view of the bridge and Manhattan skyline. The only new changes were a slapdash Van Gogh pastiche now hanging in the foyer, and the large dog bed sitting near the fire, where a long-limbed, floppy yellow dog drowsed.

Leonidas took a deep breath, dizzy with the memory of how happy he'd been here, in those

stolen hours when he'd been simply Leo, nothing more. This was enemy territory—Daisy's
home—but it somehow still felt warm. Far more
than his own multimillion-dollar homes around
the world.

He felt suddenly insecure.

"You said this is Franck Bain's apartment," he
said slowly.

"So?"

"Why has he let you stay so long? Are you
lovers?"

Closing the door behind him, Daisy said coldly,
"It's none of your business, but no. He was my
father's friend, and he is trying to help me. That's
all."

"Why would I believe that?"

"Why would you even care?" She looked at
him challengingly. "I'm sure you've had lovers by
the score since you tossed me out of your house."

But he hadn't. He hadn't had sex in five
months—not since their last time together. But
that was the last thing Leonidas wanted to admit
to Daisy. He lifted his chin. "I did not toss you
out."

"You asked me what I was still doing at your
house. And told me to go!"

"Funny, I mostly remember you insulting
me, calling me a liar and saying how badly you
wished you could hurt me." He gave a low, bitter

laugh. "I guess you figured out a way, didn't you? By not telling me you were pregnant."

The two of them stared at each other in the fading red light, an electric current of hatred sizzling the air between them.

They were so close, he thought. Their bodies could touch with the slightest movement. His gaze fell unwillingly to her lips.

He saw a shiver pass over Daisy.

"You're a bastard," she whispered.

Those were truer words than she knew. He took a deep breath, struggling to hold back his insecurity, his pain. He met her gaze evenly.

"You didn't always think so." His gaze moved toward the hallway, toward the dark shadow of her bedroom door. "When we spent hours in bed. You wanted me then. Just as I wanted you."

Her lips parted. Then she swallowed, stepping back.

"You're charming when you want to be." Her jaw hardened. "But beneath your good looks, your money, your charm—you're nothing."

You little monster. I wish you'd never been born!

In spite of his best efforts, emotion flooded through him—emotion he'd spent his whole adult life trying to outrun and prove wrong, by the company he'd built, by his massively increasing fortune, by the beautiful women he'd bedded, by his worldwide acclaim.

But Leonidas suddenly realized he would never escape it. Even with all of his fame and fortune, he was still the same worthless, unwanted boy, without a real family or home. Without a father, with a mother who despised him—raised by the twin demons of shame and grief.

He said tightly, "How you feel about me, or I feel about you, is irrelevant now. What matters is taking care of our baby."

Daisy looked at him incredulously. "I know that. Don't you think I know that? Why else do you think I tried to hide my pregnancy?"

"Don't you think our daughter needs a father?"

"Not a father like you!"

Blood rushed through his ears. With her every accusation, the stunned rage he'd felt on the river pathway built higher, making it harder to stay calm. But he managed to say evenly, "You accuse me of being a monster. All I'm trying to do is take responsibility for my child."

"How?" she cried. "By threatening me with lawyers?"

"I never actually meant—" He ground his teeth. "You were refusing to even talk to me."

"For good reason!"

"Daisy," he said quietly, "What are you so afraid of?"

She stared at him for a long moment, then looked away. He waited out her silence, until she finally said in a small voice, "I'm scared you'll try and take her from me. I saw what your money and lawyers did in court, with my father. I'm scared you'll turn them against me and try to take her—not because you love her. Out of spite. Because you can."

She really did think the worst of him. Leonidas exhaled. "I would never try to take any baby away from a loving parent. Never."

Daisy slowly looked at him, and he saw a terrible hope rising in her green eyes. "You wouldn't?"

"No. But I'm her parent, too. Whether you like it or not, we're both responsible. I never imagined I'd ever become a father, but now that she exists, I can't let her go. She's my only family in the world, do you know that?"

Silently, Daisy shook her head.

"I can't abandon her," he said. "Or risk having her wonder about me, wonder why I didn't love her enough to be there for her every day, to help raise her, to love her. To truly be her father."

Looking down at the hardwood floor, she said in a small voice, "So what can we do?"

Yes—what? How could Leonidas make sure he was part of his child's life forever, without lawyers, without threats? Without always fearing that Daisy might at any moment choose to disappear, or marry another man—a man who might always secretly despise his stepdaughter for not being his own?

His lips suddenly parted.

A simple idea. Insane. Easy. With one stroke, everything could be secure. Everything could be his.

It was an idea so crazy, he'd never imagined he would consider it. But as soon as he thought of it, the vibrating tension left his body. Leonidas suddenly felt calmer than he'd felt in days—in months.

He gave her a small smile. "Our baby needs a father. She needs a name. And I intend to give her mine." He met her gaze. "And you, as well."

She stared at him, her lovely face horrified. "What are you saying?"

"The answer is simple, Daisy." He tilted his head, looking down at her. "You're going to marry me."

CHAPTER FOUR

Marry Leonidas Niarxos?

Standing in the deepening shadows of the apartment, Daisy stared at Leonidas, her mouth open.

"Are you crazy?" she exploded. "I'm not going to marry you!"

His darkly handsome face grew cold. "We both created this child. We should both raise her." His black eyes narrowed. "I never want her to question who she is. Or feel anything less than cherished by both her parents."

"As if you could ever love anyone!" She still felt sick remembering how he'd once said, *I never claimed to love you.*

"You're right. I'm not sure I know how to love anyone." As she gaped at his honesty, Leonidas shook his head. "But I know I can protect and provide. It is my job as a man. Not just for her. Also for you."

"Why?" she whispered.

Leonidas looked down at her.

"Because I can," he said simply. He took a deep breath. "I might not have the ability to love you, Daisy. But I can take care of you. Just as I can take care of our daughter. If you'll let me."

Daisy swallowed hard.

"But, marriage…" she whispered. "How could we promise each other forever, without love?"

"Love is not necessary between us—or even desirable. Romantic love can be destructive."

Destructive? Daisy looked at his clenched jaw, the tightness around his eyes. Had someone broken Leonidas's heart? She fought the impulse to reach out to him, to ask questions, to offer comfort. Sympathy was the last thing she wanted to feel right now.

"What about marrying someone you despise?" she pointed out. "That seems pretty destructive."

"Do you really hate me so much, Daisy? Just because I was afraid to tell you my last name when we met? Just because, when a man tried to sell me a forgery, I pressed charges? For that, you're determined to hate me for the rest of your life? No matter what that does to our child?"

She bit her lip. When he put it like that…

Her heart was pounding. She thought of how she'd felt last October, when she'd loved him, and he'd broken her heart. It would kill her if that ever happened again. "I can't love you again."

"Good." Leonidas looked down at her in the

falling light. "I'm not asking you to. But give me a chance to win back your trust."

Her heart lifted to her throat. Trust?

It was a cruel reminder of how she'd once trusted Leo, blindly believing him to be perfect. How could she ever trust him again?

Daisy looked down at her short waterproof boots. "I don't know if I can."

"Why won't you try?" His face was in shadow. He tilted his head. "Are you in love with someone else? The artist who owns this apartment, Franck Bain?"

"I told you, he's a friend, nothing more!" Daisy kept Franck's marriage proposal to herself. No point in giving Leonidas ammunition. She shook her head fiercely. "I don't want to love anyone. Not anymore. I've given up on that fairy tale since—"

Her voice cut off, but it was too late.

Leonidas drew closer. The light from the hallway caressed the hard edges of his face. "Since you loved me?"

A shiver went through Daisy. Against her will, her gaze fell to his cruel, sensual lips. She still couldn't forget the memory of his kiss, his mouth so hot against her skin, making her whole body come alive.

No, she told herself angrily. No! She'd allowed her body to override her brain once before. And look what had happened!

But she still felt Leonidas's every movement. His every breath. Even though he didn't touch her, she could still feel him, blood and bone.

He looked down at her. "You don't need to worry, then," he said softly. "Because we agree. Neither of us is seeking love. Because romantic love is destructive."

She agreed with him, didn't she? So why did her heart twist a little as she said, "Yes, I guess you're right." She took a deep breath. "That doesn't mean I can just forgive or forget what you did."

"You loved your father."

"Yes."

"He meant everything to you."

"Yes!"

Leonidas looked at her. "Don't you think our daughter deserves the chance to have a father, too?"

She caught her breath.

Was she being selfish? Putting her own anger ahead of their baby's best interests—not just financially, but emotionally?

"How can I know you'll be a good father to our daughter?" she said in a small voice.

"I swear it to you. On my honor."

"Your *honor*," she said bitterly. Her hands went protectively over her baby bump, over her cotton shirt.

He gently put his larger hand over hers.

"Yes. My honor. Which means a great deal to me." He looked her straight in the eye. "I have no family, Daisy. No siblings or cousins. Both my parents are dead. I never intended to marry or have a child of my own. But now... This baby is all I have. All I care about is her happiness. I will do anything to protect her."

Daisy heard the words for the vow they were. Her heart lifted to her throat. He truly wanted to be a good father. She heard it in his voice. He cared about this child in a way she'd never expected.

Her heart suddenly ached. How she wished she could believe him! How lovely it would be to actually have a partner in her pregnancy, someone else looking out for her, rather than having to figure out everything herself!

But could she live with a man who'd done what Leonidas had done? Even if she never loved him—could she live with him? Accept him as her co-parent—trust him as a friend?

His hand tightened over hers. "There could be other benefits to our marriage, Daisy," he said huskily. "More than just being partners. Living together, we could have other...pleasures."

He was talking about sharing a bed. Images of their lovemaking flashed through her, and she felt a bead of sweat between her breasts.

"If you think I'm falling into bed with you, you're crazy," she said desperately. She stepped back, pulling away from his touch. Just to make sure she didn't do something she'd regret, like reach for his strong, powerful body, pull it against her own, and lift her lips to his…

She couldn't. She mustn't!

"I can't forget how it felt to make love to you," he said in a low voice. "I still dream about it. Do you?"

"No," she lied.

His dark eyes glinted. His lips curved wickedly as he came forward, and without warning, he swept her up into his powerful arms.

"Shall I remind you what it was like?" he said softly, his gaze hot against her trembling lips.

For a moment, standing in this apartment where they'd made love so many times, in so many locations—on that sofa, against that wall—all she wanted was to kiss him, to feel his hands against her naked skin. It terrified her, how easily he made her body yearn to surrender!

But if she did, how long would it take before she gave him everything?

Trembling, she wrenched away. "No."

He looked at her, and she thought she saw a flash of vulnerability in his dark eyes. Then his handsome face hardened. "I'm not going away, Daisy. I'm not going to abandon her."

"I know." She prayed he didn't realize how close she was to spinning out of control. She needed to get him out of here, out of this apartment with all its painfully joyful memories. "I'm tired. Can we talk tomorrow?"

"No," he said, unyielding. "This needs to be settled."

Sunny rose from her dog bed to sniff curiously at Leonidas. The dog looked up at him with hopeful eyes, clearly waiting to be petted. He briefly scratched her ears. As he straightened, the dog licked his hand.

Traitor. Daisy glared at her pet. Just when she most wanted her canine protector to growl and bark, another female fell helplessly at the Greek tycoon's feet!

Leonidas stood before her, illuminated by the bright Manhattan skyline and the starry night, and a lump rose in her throat. Did he know how memories of their love affair haunted her?

If it had been Leo wanting to kiss her, she would have already fallen into his arms. If it had been Leo proposing, she would have married him in an instant.

But it wasn't. Instead, it was a handsome stranger, a coldhearted billionaire, the man who'd put her father in jail.

"I can see you're tired," Leonidas said gently, looking at her slumped shoulders and the way her hands cradled her belly. "Are you hungry? Perhaps I could take you to dinner?"

He sounded hesitant, as if he were expecting her to refuse. But after her early morning shift at the diner, followed by her checkup at the obstetrician's office and then walking her energetic dog, Daisy *was* tired and hungry.

"Another fancy restaurant?" she said.

"Whatever kind of restaurant you want. Homey. Casual." Leonidas smiled down at Sunny, who was by now licking his hand and flirtatiously holding up her paw. He added, "You can even bring your dog." He straightened, giving her a slow-rising, sensual smile. "What do you say?"

It was really not fair to use her dog against her. Or that smile, which burned right through her. Daisy hated how her body reacted to Leonidas's smile, causing electricity to course through her veins. She was no better than her pet, she thought in disgust.

But she *was* hungry. And more than anything, she wanted to get Leonidas out of this apartment, with all its sensual memories, before she did something she'd regret.

"Fine," she bit out. "Dinner. Just dinner, mind. Someplace homey and casual. Where dogs are allowed."

Leonidas's smile became a grin. "I know just the place."

Leonidas looked at Daisy, sitting next to him in the back seat of the Rolls-Royce. Daisy's floppy yellow dog was in her lap, sticking her head excitedly out the window. The animal's tongue lolled out of her mouth as they crossed over the East River, into Manhattan.

Sadly, the pet's mistress didn't seem nearly so pleased. Daisy's lovely face was troubled as she stared fiercely out the window.

But it was enough. He'd convinced Daisy to come to dinner. He'd given quiet instructions to his chauffeur, Jenkins, and sent a text to his assistant. Everything was set.

Now he had Daisy, he never intended to let her go.

It was strange. Leonidas had never imagined wanting to get married, and certainly never imagined becoming a father. But now he was determined to do both and do them well. In spite of—or even perhaps because of—his own awful childhood.

For his whole life, he'd been driven to prove himself. His first memories involved desperately trying to please the man he thought was his father, who called him stupid and useless. Leonidas had tried to do better, to make his penmanship, his English conjugations, his skill with an épée all perfect. But no matter his efforts, Giannis had bullied him and sneered at him, while his mother ignored him completely—unless they were in company. Appearances were all that mattered, and as violently as his parents fought each other, they were united in wanting others to believe they had the perfect marriage, the perfect son, the perfect family.

But the truth was far from perfect. His parents had seemed to hate each other—but not as much as they hated Leonidas. From the age of five, when he'd first noticed that other children were hugged and loved and praised by their parents, Leonidas had known something was horribly wrong with him. There had to be, or why would his own parents despise him, no matter how hard he tried?

He'd never managed to impress them. When he was fourteen, they'd died, leaving him with no one but distant trustees, and boarding school in America.

At twenty-one, fresh out of Princeton, he'd seized the reins of Giannis's failing leather goods business, near bankruptcy after seven years of being run into the ground by trustees. He decided he didn't need a family. He didn't need love. Success would be the thing to prove his worth to the world.

And he'd done what no one expected of an heir: he'd rebuilt the company from the ground up. He'd renamed it Liontari, and over the next fifteen years, he'd made it a global empire through will and work and luck. He'd fought his way through business acquisitions, hostile takeovers, and created, through blood and sweat, the worldwide conglomerate now headquartered in New York.

But none of those battles, none of those hard-won multimillion-dollar deals, had ever made him feel as triumphant as Daisy agreeing to dinner tonight.

This was personal.

Leonidas had never been promiscuous with love affairs, having only a few short-term relationships each year, but the women in his life had often accused him of being cold, even soulless. "You have no feelings at all!" was an accusation that had been hurled at him more than once.

And it was probably true. He tended to intellectualize everything. He didn't *feel* things like everyone else seemed to. Even when he beat down business rivals, he didn't glory in the triumph. Losing a lover made him shrug, not weep.

But he told himself he was lucky. Without feelings, he could be rational, rather than pursuing emotional wild goose chases as others did. The only emotion he really knew was anger, and he kept even that in check when he could.

Except when he'd been Leo.

It was strange, looking back. For the month he'd been Daisy's lover, it had been exhilarating to let down his guard and not have to live up to the world's expectations of Leonidas Niarxos, billionaire playboy. In Daisy's eyes, he'd been an ordinary man, a nobody, really—but somehow she'd still thought him worthy.

And he'd loved it. He'd been free to be truly

himself, instead of always being primed for battle, ready to attack or defend. He'd been able to show his silly side, like the time they'd nearly died laughing together while digging through vintage vinyl albums at a Brooklyn record shop, teasing each other about whose taste in music was worse. Or the time they'd brought weird flavors of ice cream home from an artisanal shop, and they'd ended up smearing each other with all the different flavors—chocolate cinnamon, whiskey banana and even one oddly tart sugar dill... He shivered, remembering how it had tasted to suckle that exotic flavor off Daisy's bare, taut nipple.

In the back of his mind, Leonidas had always known it could not last.

But this would.

He would marry Daisy. They'd raise their child together. Their daughter would have a different childhood than Leonidas had had. She would always feel wanted. Cherished. Encouraged. Whether she was making mud pies or learning calculus or kicking soccer balls, whether she was succeeding or failing, she would always know that her father adored her.

But marriage was the key to that stability. Otherwise, what would stop Daisy from someday becoming another man's wife? Leonidas wanted to be a full-time father, not a part-time one. He wanted a stable home, and for their daughter to always know exactly who her family was. And if Daisy married someone else, how could he guarantee that any other man could care for Leonidas's child as she needed—as she deserved?

He had to be there for his child. And Daisy.

He had to convince her that he was right.

But how?

Leonidas looked at Daisy, sitting next to him in the spacious back seat of the limo. Convincing her to join him for dinner was a good start. But as they crossed into Manhattan, she still stared fiercely out the window, stroking her dog as if it were an emotional support animal. Her lower lip wobbled, as if she were fighting back tears.

The smile slid away from Leonidas's face. A marriage where the husband and wife fought in white-knuckled warfare, or secretly despised each other in a cold war, was the last thing he wanted. He'd seen that in his own parents, though they'd supposedly once been passionately in love.

He wanted a partnership with Daisy. A friendship. That was the best way to create a home for a child. At least so he'd heard.

Leonidas took a deep breath. He had to woo Daisy. Win her. Convince her he was worthy of her trust and esteem, if not her love. Just as he'd done with Liontari—he had to take their bankrupt, desolate relationship, and make it the envy of the world.

But how?

As the Rolls-Royce crossed into the shadowy canyons between Manhattan's illuminated skyscrapers, the moonlight was pale above them. The limo finally pulled up in front of his five-story mansion in the West Village. Daisy looked up through her car window.

"You call that homey?" she said in a low voice.

He shrugged. "It's home. And very dog friendly."

"Since when?"

"Since now." Getting out of the car, Leonidas shook his head at his driver, and opened her door himself.

But as Daisy got out of the back seat, she wouldn't meet Leonidas's eyes, or take his offered hand. Cuddling her dog against her chest, she looked up at Leonidas's hundred-year-old brownstone, her lovely face anxious.

"I'm not sure this is a good idea."

"It's just dinner. A totally casual, very homey, dog-friendly dinner."

Her expression was dubious, but she got out of the car. Daisy and her dog followed him slowly up the steps to the door, where he punched in the code. They went into the foyer, beneath crystal chandeliers high overhead.

"Where's the butler?" she asked, the corners of her lips curving up slightly as he helped her take off her long black coat.

"He quit a few months ago."

"Quit?"

"I've been living in Paris. He went in search of less boring employment." He shrugged. "I still have Mrs. Berry and a few other staffers, but they've all gone home for the night."

Daisy drew back, her face troubled in the shadowy foyer. "So we're alone?"

He took off his coat, adding it to the nearby closet beside hers. "Is that a problem?"

Her gaze slid away. "Of course not. I'm not scared of you."

"Good. You're safe with me, Daisy. Don't you realize that? Don't you realize I would die to protect you—you and the baby?"

Her eyes met his. "You would?"

"I told you. Our baby is my only family. That means you're under my protection as well. I will always protect and provide for you. On my honor." Remembering how little she'd thought of his honor, he added quietly, "On my life."

As their eyes locked, the air between them electrified. Her gaze fell to his lips. His hand tightened on her shoulder as he moved closer—

The doorbell rang behind them, jarring him. Then he smiled. "That must be dinner."

She looked surprised. "You ordered takeout?"

"My housekeeper's gone home. How else could I serve dinner? I swore to protect you, not poison you with burned meals."

The edges of her mouth lifted. "True."

For a moment, they smiled at each other, and he knew she was remembering the single disastrous night he'd tried to cook for her in the Brooklyn apartment. Somehow he'd turned boiled spaghetti noodles and canned marinara sauce into a full-scale culinary disaster that had required a fire extinguisher.

Then her smile fell, and he knew that she was thinking of everything that had happened since.

That was a battle he could not win. So he turned to answer the door. Speaking quietly to the delivery person, he took the bags, then turned to face Daisy. "Shall we?"

She looked at the bags. "What is it?"

"Chinese." He hesitated. "I know it used to be your favorite, but if you'd rather have something else…"

"Kung pao chicken?" she interrupted.

"Of course."

"It's exactly what I want." She looked almost dismayed about it.

Leonidas led her through the large, spacious house to a back hallway which led to an enormous kitchen, her dog's nails clicking against the marble floor as she followed behind. On the other side of the kitchen was a small, cozy breakfast room with wide windows and French doors overlooking a private courtyard.

Outside, in the moonlight, a few snowflakes were falling. As Leonidas put the bags of Chinese takeout on the breakfast table, Daisy looked out at the courtyard in surprise. "You have your own yard? In the middle of Manhattan?"

Leonidas shrugged. "It's why I bought this house. I always want fresh air and space."

Daisy's forehead furrowed. "*You* like fresh air?"

He barked a laugh. "Is that so shocking?"

"I just picture you only in boardrooms, or society ballrooms, or the back seat of a Rolls-Royce or..."

"Let me guess," he responded, amused. "Sitting in the basement of a bank, counting my piles of gold like Scrooge McDuck?"

Her green eyes widened at mention of the old cartoon character. "How do you know who that is?" she said accusingly. "Do you have a child?"

She really did believe the worst of him. His smile faded. "No, but I was one."

"In Greece?"

"I was sent to an American boarding school at nine."

Daisy blinked, her face horrified. "Your parents sent you away? At *nine*?"

"They did me a favor. Believe me." Turning away, he went back to the big gleaming kitchen and grabbed two plates and two bowls, china edged with twenty-four-carat gold. He placed the plates on the table, and the bowls on the marble floor.

Taking three bottles of water from the small refrigerator beneath the side table, he poured water into one of the bowls. Her dog came forward eagerly.

"Are you crazy?" Daisy looked incredulously at her dog lapping water from the gold-edged china bowl. "Don't you have any cheap dishes?"

"No. Sorry."

"We're going to need some, before—" She cut herself off.

"Before our baby needs a plate?" Tilting his head, he looked down at her. "I'm looking forward to it," he said softly. "All of it. I'd like this house to be your home, Daisy. Yours and the baby's. Make it your own. Whatever you want, your slightest desire, it will be yours."

She looked at him with wide stricken eyes, then changed the subject, turning away to stare at a painting on the opposite wall. "You like modern art."

"Yes," he said cautiously.

"Do you own any of Franck's?"

Leonidas snorted. "He's overrated. I don't know anyone who owns his paintings."

"Well, lots of people must buy them, because he's very successful. He travels first class around the world." She tilted her head. "Everyone loves him."

"Everyone including you?" he said unwillingly.

Daisy looked at him in surprise. "Are you jealous?"

"Maybe."

"You were never jealous before."

He shrugged. "That was before."

"Before?"

"Before you stopped looking at me like you used to." He did miss it, the way Daisy used to look at him. As if he were the whole world to her, Christmas and her birthday all at once. It was a shock to realize that. He'd thought he didn't care if Daisy loved him. In fact, after what he'd seen his parents go through, he'd convinced himself that romantic love was a liability.

But he missed having her love him.

"That was a long time ago," Daisy mumbled, her cheeks red. She reached over to scratch Sunny's ears. "Before I found out the man I loved was just a dream."

Leonidas looked down, realizing that his hands were trembling. "We can find a new dream together."

"A new dream?"

"A partnership. Family. Respect."

"Maybe." Daisy tried to smile. "I don't know. But I've lost dreams before. Did I ever tell you how thoroughly I failed when I tried to become an artist?"

"No."

"I didn't sell a single painting. Not even a pity sale." Her cheeks colored. "I don't expect you to understand what it feels like. I'm sure you've never failed at anything."

"You feel empty. Helpless. Like there's nothing you can do, and nothing will ever change for you."

She looked at him in surprise. He gave her a small, tight smile, then started unpacking the takeout cartons from the bags. "I asked my housekeeper to get organic dog food. It's in the kitchen." He quirked a dark eyebrow. "Unless Sunny would prefer kung pao chicken, too?"

"You're hilarious." But Daisy's expression softened as she looked at him. "Sunny already ate. She's fine for now."

"As you wish." As he pulled out carton after carton from the bags, she looked incredulous.

"Will there be a crowd joining us?"

"I wasn't sure if you might be having pregnancy cravings, so I got a little of everything. As well as double of the kung pao." Leonidas handed her a plate, which she swiftly filled with food. He gave her a napkin and chopsticks from the bag, and a bottle of water. He made himself a plate, then sat beside her at the table.

But the truth was, he didn't care about food. He was more interested in watching her.

As they ate, they spoke of inconsequential things, about anything and everything but the obvious. He was mesmerized, watching her eat everything on her plate, then go back for more.

Everything about Daisy drew him—not just her body, her pregnancy-swollen breasts, or the curve of her belly. Everything. The way she drew the chopsticks back slowly from her lips. The flutter of her dark lashes against her cheeks. The graceful swoop of her neck before it disappeared beneath the white cotton collar of her shirt. Her thick brown hair falling in waves over her shoulders. Even her voice, as she teased him about the fundraiser he'd held last year, because his favored politician had lost.

He looked at her. "Will you stay with me?" he asked quietly. "At least until the baby is born?"

Her seafoam green eyes pulled him into the waves, like a siren luring him to drown.

"It's not that simple," she said.

"I know. For you, it is not. But it is for me." Folding his hands, he leaned forward. "Give me the chance to earn your trust. And show you that I can be the partner you need. That our baby needs."

Her cheeks burned red beneath his gaze. He felt out of his element. He knew he should probably play it cool. Act cold. Manipulate, seize control.

But for the first time in his adult life, he could not. Not now. Not with her.

All he could do was ask.

Daisy looked away. "I'm planning to move to California in September. For nursing school."

"Why? You don't need to work." The thought of her moving three thousand miles away chilled him. "I will always support you."

"What if you change your mind?" She snorted. "Do you expect me to just give myself up to your hands?"

An erotic image went through him of his hands stroking her naked body. He took a deep breath. "At least stay with me until September. Let me take care of you while you're pregnant. Give me a chance to bond with our daughter after she's born. Then you can see how you feel."

She bit her lip. "Stay here through the summer?"

He could feel her weakening. "As long as you like. Either way, you and the baby will never worry about money again."

"I'm not asking you to support me, Leonidas."

"You're the mother of my child. I will always provide for you. It's my job as a man." Looking down at her, he said quietly, "You would not try to deny me that."

She chewed her lip uncertainly, then sighed. "I guess I could stay until September. If you're sure you really want me here that long?"

"I'm sure," he said automatically.

"Three months living with a pregnant woman? A whole summer with a crying baby? That won't cramp your style?"

"It's what I want."

"Well." She gave a reluctant smile. "I've imposed on Franck's charity long enough. I might as well impose on you for a while."

"It's no imposition. I want to marry you."

She looked away. Her cheeks burned as she mumbled, "So does he."

Leonidas gaped. "What!"

Daisy rolled her eyes. "It was a pity proposal. He felt sorry for me."

Leonidas doubted pity had anything to do with it. "Did he try to kiss you?"

She looked shocked. "*Kiss* me? Of course not—Franck is old enough to be my father!" But Leonidas saw sudden uneasiness in her eyes, and he wondered exactly what Franck Bain had said to her. He made a mental note to keep the middle-aged artist on his radar.

He was furious that another man had made a move on her. How dared he? She was carrying Leonidas's baby!

But could he blame Bain for wanting her? Any man would want Daisy. It made Leonidas all the more determined to marry her, and claim her as his own.

She tilted her head, looking up at him through dark lashes. "At least you have good reason to want me here. You love our baby." She paused. "I never expected that."

Relief flooded through him. "So you'll stay?"

"With one condition." She lifted her chin. "You

have to promise, when I want to leave, you'll let me go."

He saw there was no arguing with her on this point. He hesitated. Once Daisy was here, living in his house, he believed he'd soon convince her they should marry. They both loved their baby. That was a good enough reason.

He hoped.

"If you'll promise," he said slowly, "you'll never try to keep me from my daughter. Or hide her from me, even if you leave New York."

Biting her lip, she gave a single nod.

Leonidas held out his hand. "Then I agree."

"Me too." Daisy shook his hand. He felt the slow burn of her palm against his, before she quickly drew it away.

"What changed your mind?" he asked quietly.

She looked up at him. "I loved my dad. That was what convinced me. Because you're right. How could I deny our daughter the same chance for a father?"

The father that Daisy had lost, because of him. Leonidas felt a lump in his throat. The ghost of Patrick Cassidy would always be between them. How would they ever get past it?

He said in a low voice, "Will you stay tonight?"

"Yes. So will Sunny. Where I go, my dog goes."

"She's very welcome. Like I said. We're dog

friendly." Looking at the dog lazing nearby, he added, "Besides, I think she likes me."

"I noticed," she said wryly. She yawned. "Though I didn't pack any clothes."

"I can send someone back—"

"Wake up one of your employees to send them to Brooklyn and back? I'm not that evil. I'll just sleep naked."

Leonidas broke out in a hot sweat, remembering her bare body against his, the soft sweetness of her skin as she moved against him. He wondered what it would feel like to touch her now, what she looked like naked, so heavily pregnant with his child...

No! He forced the image from his mind. He couldn't seduce her. Not yet. She was still skittish, looking for an excuse to flee. He couldn't give her one. He had to take his time. He had to win her trust.

"Fine. We can pick up your things tomorrow," he said, breathing deeply.

"There's not much to collect." She gave a brief smile. "You don't have to help me. I can just take the subway over."

"Leave you to struggle with suitcases and boxes on the subway? Forget it. I'm helping you."

"Fine," she sighed. She yawned again. "I think I need to go to bed."

He tried not to think about her in bed. "Sure."

"I just need to let Sunny out first." She rose

to her feet, opening the door for her dog, who quickly bounded out into the courtyard.

As she stood in the doorway, Leonidas couldn't stop his gaze from lingering over her belly and full, swollen breasts, imagining them beneath her white shirt and black leggings. Turning back, she caught his gaze. He blushed like a guilty teenager.

Clearing his throat, he gathered up the takeout bags and trash, leaving the plates in one of the kitchen sinks. A moment later, after Sunny returned from outside, Leonidas said in a low voice, "I'll show you to your room."

He led her through the kitchen, the dog following them down the hall and up the sweeping staircase to the second floor.

As they passed, Daisy glanced nervously at his master bedroom, where they'd had their blowout fight last autumn. But he didn't pause. He led her to the best guest room.

Reaching inside, he turned on the light, revealing a beautiful suite, elegantly decorated in cream and light pink. "There's an en suite bathroom. All stocked with toothbrushes and toiletries and anything else you might require."

"Do you often have guests?" she asked, smiling awkwardly as her dog went ahead to sniff, scouting out the bedroom.

"You're the first," he said honestly. "Mrs. Berry always seemed to think someone might come to visit. Even though I told her I have no family."

"Had," Daisy said. "Now you do."

His heart twisted strangely. "Right. Good night."

"Thank you," she said softly.

He turned back to face her, standing at the door. "Thanks for staying."

She licked her lips nervously. "Leonidas, you know that…even if someday I agree to marry you, far in the future…and I'm not saying I will…but…"

"But?"

"You know I'll never be yours again. Not like I was."

Never? Leonidas could still remember how she'd felt in his arms. Soft. Sensual. Making love to her had been like fire. And now she was pregnant with his child. Her body was even more lush, with a rounded belly beneath full breasts. He wanted to see her. To feel her. He was hard just thinking about it.

Reaching out, Leonidas cupped her cheek. Her skin felt warm and soft, so soft. "I will do everything I can to win you back," he said softly. "In every way. And soon…"

For a moment, he was lost in the maelstrom of her velvety black pupils. His gaze fell to her full pink lips. He forgot his earlier vow not to seduce her in his thundering need to kiss her, and claim what was his, after months of agonizing desire.

Slowly, he lowered his head—

Daisy jerked back violently. "No." Her eyes were luminous with sudden tears. "No!"

And she slammed the bedroom door in his face.

CHAPTER FIVE

LEONIDAS DID NOT sleep well.

He tossed and turned, picturing the woman he wanted sleeping in the next room down the hall. So close, and yet she might as well have been a million miles away.

Finally, he saw the early gray light of dawn through the window. Rising wearily from bed in his boxers, he stretched his tired, aching body, as the cool air of the room invigorated his muscles, from his shoulders to his chest and thighs. Going to the window, he pushed open heavy white curtains. Below, he saw the quiet West Village street was covered with a dusting of white. Snow had fallen during the night.

Leonidas's hand tightened on the white curtains. He was furious with himself. Why had he tried to kiss her? How had he ever thought that would be a good idea, in their relationship's current fragile state?

He hadn't been thinking. At all. That was the problem.

He'd let his desire for Daisy override everything else. The stakes were so high. He had to make her feel comfortable here, so she would remain. So they could become friends. Partners. *Married*. For their baby's sake.

Instead, he could still hear the echo of her door, slamming in his face.

How could he have been so stupid? Frustration pounded through him.

Pulling on exercise shorts and a T-shirt from his walk-in closet, Leonidas dug out his running shoes. He peeked down the darkened hallway and saw Daisy's door was closed. He didn't even hear her dog. He wondered how she'd slept.

After going downstairs, Leonidas went out into the gray dawn and went on a five-mile run to clear his head. With most of the city still asleep, he relished the quiet, the only sound his shoes crunching in the thin layer of snow.

Daisy had such a warm heart. He'd seen it in her devotion to her father, to her friends—and their devotion to her. Her kindness. Her loyalty.

He had to win her trust. Prove to her he could deserve it. Even if that meant he had to wait a long time to make love to her.

Even if that meant he had to wait forever.

He could do it. He was strong enough to fight his own desire. He *could*.

Returning home with a clear head and a determined will, he ran upstairs, taking the steps two at a time. He paused when he saw Daisy's door open. But her bedroom was empty. Had she already gone downstairs? Could she have left? Fled the city in the night—

No. He took a steadying breath. She'd promised she'd never try to keep his child from him. And he believed in her word.

But still. He wanted to find her. Going to his en suite bathroom, he quickly showered and dressed in a sleek black suit with a gray button-up shirt. The Liontari corporate office had recently loosened up the dress code, allowing men to skip ties and suits, though of course, the creatives and designers of the specific luxury clothing brands played by their own rules.

But Leonidas had his own strict rule, to always represent the best his company had to offer. And so, he always wore the same cut of suit from his favorite men's brand, Xerxes, altered to fit his unusually broad shoulders, biceps and thighs. He checked the clock. He always had breakfast around seven; he was expected at work in an hour. The thought gave him little pleasure.

Going downstairs, he couldn't find either Daisy or Sunny. Phyllis Berry, his longtime housekeeper, was cooking eggs and sizzling bacon in the kitchen, as she always was this time of the morning.

"Good morning, sir."

"Good morning, Mrs. Berry." Sitting at the

breakfast table as usual, he hesitated. "I don't suppose you've seen—"

"Miss Cassidy?" The petite white-haired woman beamed at him as she dished up a plate. "Yes. And all I can say is—finally!"

"Finally?"

"Finally, you're settling down. Such a nice girl, too. And pregnant! You wasted no time!" With a chuckle, she brought the plate of bacon and eggs, along with a cup of black coffee, and put them down on the table in front of him with a wistful sigh. "I can hardly wait to have a baby about the place. The pitter-patter of little feet. And a dog! I must admit I'm surprised. But better late than never, Mr. Niarxos. After all these years, you finally took my advice!"

Raising his eyebrows, Leonidas sipped hot coffee, while he was pretending to skim the business news. "You met Daisy?"

"Yes, about a half hour ago, when she left to walk her dog. Such a lovely girl." Mrs. Berry sighed, then gave him a severe look before she turned away. "Why you still haven't asked her to marry you is something I don't understand. Young people today…"

Leonidas's lips curved upward. *Young person?* He was thirty-five. But then, Mrs. Berry, who'd worked for Leonidas for many years, regarded her employer with a proprietary eye. She seemed to regard him as the grandson she'd never had, and never hesitated to tell him the error of his ways.

He heard the slam of the front door, the dog's nails clacking against the marble floor, and the soft murmur of Daisy's voice, greeting some unseen member of his house staff down the hall. Trust Daisy to already have made friends.

Her dog, no longer a puppy in size but clearly very much in temperament, bounded into the kitchen first, her tongue lolling, her big paws tracking ice and snow from her walk. Mrs. Berry took one look and blanched. She moved at supersonic speed, picking the animal up off the floor. But her wrinkled face was indulgent as she looked down at the dog.

"Let's get you into the mudroom," she said affectionately. "And after we clean your paws, we'll get you properly fed." The dog gave her a slobbery kiss. Mrs. Berry smiled at Daisy, who'd followed her pet into the kitchen. "If that's all right with you, Miss Cassidy."

"Of course. Oh, dear. I'm so sorry!" Daisy glanced with dismay at the tracks her dog had made on the previously spotless floor. "I'm afraid it's a great deal of trouble—"

"No trouble at all," Mrs. Berry said, with a purposeful glance at Leonidas. The crafty old lady was leaving them alone. He wondered irritably if she expected, as soon as she left the room, for him to immediately go down on one knee in front of Daisy and pull a diamond ring out of his pocket? He would have done so gladly, if it would have done any good!

"Good morning, Leonidas." Daisy's voice was shy. She was, of course, wearing the same clothes from yesterday, her long black coat unzipped over her belly. "I saw you come back from my window. Were you running?"

"It helps me relax."

"Does it?" She snorted. "You should walk my dog sometime, then. She'd probably love running with you. She has more energy than I do these days, always tugging at the leash!"

He furrowed his brow. "Is walking her a problem? I could get one of my staff to handle the chore…"

"Chore?" She looked at him incredulously. "It's not a chore. She's my dog. I like walking her. I just thought *she* might like running with *you*."

"Oh." He cleared his throat. "Sure. I could take her running with me." He pictured Daisy walking around the streets of New York in the darkness of early morning, and suddenly didn't like it. "Or I could come walking with you, if you want. Either way."

She blinked. "Really? That wouldn't be too much of a…a chore for you?"

"Not at all. I like her." Leonidas looked up from the table. "And I like you."

She bit her lip. He saw dark circles under her eyes. Apparently she hadn't slept very well either.

"Sit down." Rising to his feet, he pulled out a chair at the table. "Can I get you some breakfast? Are you hungry?"

She shook her head. A smile played about her full pink lips. "Mrs. Berry already made me eat some toast and fruit before she'd let me take the dog out."

Score one for Mrs. Berry. "Good." He paused awkwardly, still standing across from her. "How are you feeling?"

Her lovely face looked unhappy. Her hands clasped together as she blurted out, "I think we've made a big mistake."

Danger clanged through him. "A mistake?"

She tucked a loose tendril of brown hair behind her ear. She said softly, "I don't think I can stay here."

Leonidas stared at her in consternation. Then he understood.

"Because I almost kissed you last night," he guessed grimly. She nodded, not meeting his eyes.

He had to soothe her—make her feel safe. He took a deep breath. Going against all his instincts, he didn't move. Instead, he said gently, "You have no reason to be afraid of me."

"I'm not afraid of you. I'm afraid of—"

She cut off her words.

"Afraid of what?"

Her pale green eyes lifted to his, and he knew, no matter how Daisy tried to pretend otherwise, that she felt the same electricity. Every time her gaze fell to his lips. Every time their eyes met, and she nervously looked away. Every time he touched her and felt her tremble.

She was afraid of herself. Of her own desire. Afraid, if she gave in, that she would be lost forever.

And she was poised to flee. If he didn't reassure her, he'd scare her straight back into Franck Bain's apartment—if not his arms.

Taking a deep breath, he said, "What if I promise I won't try to kiss you?"

Silence crackled as they faced each other in the breakfast nook. Outside in the courtyard, there was a soft thump as snow fell from the branches onto the white-covered earth.

"Would you really make that promise?" she said finally.

"Yes. I'll never try to kiss you, Daisy. Not unless you want me to."

"On your honor?"

He tried to comfort himself with the fact that at least she now believed he *had* honor. "Yes."

Daisy bit her lip, then said slowly, "All right. If I have your word, then…then I'll stay."

He exhaled. "Good." He tried not to think

about how hard it would be not to kiss her. How hard it was not to kiss her even now.

He took a deep breath. "I need to go to work today."

"Work?"

"I'm CEO and principal shareholder of Liontari."

"That's a store?"

"An international consortium of brands. You've probably heard of them. Vertigris, for instance."

"What's that?"

"Champagne."

"No. But I don't really drink…"

He was surprised. Vertigris was as globally famous as Cristal or Dom Perignon. "Ridenbaugh Watches? Helios Diamonds? Cialov Handbags?"

Looking bemused, Daisy shook her head.

And all of Leonidas's plans to go into the office flew out the window. He set his jaw. "Okay. I'm taking you out."

"Out?"

"We'll collect your clothes from Bain's apartment, as I promised. Then I'm taking you to a few shops." When she frowned, still looking bewildered, he added, "We can buy a few things."

"What kind of things?"

"For your pregnancy. For the baby."

"You don't need to buy me stuff."

"Think of it as you helping *me*," he said lightly.

"Market research. You're a totally virgin consumer. I'd like your take on my brands."

Her cheeks colored at the word *virgin*. "I don't see how my opinion would be useful to you."

"It would be. But more than that, I'd really like you to understand what I do." He gave her a brief smile. "Isn't that what you were asking me? To understand my world?"

"That was before…"

"There was so much I never was able to show you before. We spent our whole time together in Brooklyn." He paused. "Let me show you Manhattan."

Her light green gaze looked troubled, then she bit her lip. "I'm not sure I can leave Sunny alone here…"

"Mrs. Berry can watch her. She's good with dogs." At least, she'd seemed good with Sunny just now. He'd never really thought about it. He'd certainly never lived with a dog before. His parents had despised the idea of pets. "She's very trustworthy." That at least was true.

He could see Daisy weighing that, and wondered if she was setting such a high bar for who was allowed to watch her dog, would any potential babysitter for their daughter need two PhDs and a letter of reference from the Dalai Lama?

"I suppose," she said finally. "As long as we're not gone for too long."

Reaching out, he took her left hand in his own,

running his thumb over her bare ring finger. "We could go to Helios," he said casually. "Look at engagement rings."

He felt her shiver and saw the flash of vulnerability in her eyes. Then she pulled her hand away.

"No," she said firmly. "No rings."

Couldn't blame a man for trying. "There must be something you need, you or the baby."

She tilted her head, then sighed, resting her hand on her swelling belly peeking out from the open black puffy coat. "I suppose it would be nice to get a new coat," she admitted. "This morning, I suddenly couldn't zip it up anymore."

As she rubbed her belly, he saw a flash of cleavage at the neckline of her white button-down shirt, and he wondered what touching those breasts would feel like. A very dangerous thing to wonder. He couldn't think about seducing her. Because he was the kind of man that if he let himself think about something, he would soon take action to achieve it.

"But you don't need to pay for it," she said quickly. Inwardly, he sighed. He'd never had so much trouble convincing a woman to let him buy her things. "While we're at Franck's," she continued, "I need to pick up my waitress uniform. I have a shift tomorrow."

Leonidas frowned. "You're not thinking of going back to work at the diner?"

"Of course." Daisy frowned. "Do you really

think I'd just quit my job? And leave my boss in the lurch?"

"Why would you—" Gritting his teeth, he said, "You don't have to be a waitress anymore. Ever. I will take care of you!"

She put her hand on her hip. "Are you telling me not to work?"

Raising his eyebrow, he countered, "Are you telling *me* it's comfortable to stand on your feet all day, when you're this pregnant?"

Daisy's expression became uncertain, and her hand fell to her side. "I'll think about it," she said finally. "On the drive to Brooklyn." She paused. "Actually, could we…um…take the subway or something?"

"You don't like the Rolls-Royce?"

She rolled her eyes. "It's a *limo*. With a uniformed driver."

"So?"

"Well, the whole thing's a little bit much, isn't it?"

As much as he wanted to please her, Leonidas wasn't quite ready for the subway. They compromised by having his driver, Jenkins—wearing street clothes, not his uniform—take them in Leonidas's Range Rover.

When the two of them arrived at the Brooklyn co-op overlooking the river, the building's doorman greeted Daisy with a warm smile, then glared at Leonidas.

"You all right, Miss Cassidy?" the man asked her.

She gave him a sweet smile. "Yes. Thank you, Walter." She glanced at Leonidas, clearly enjoying his discomfiture.

"Thank you, Walter," he echoed. The man scowled back. Obviously their last meeting, when Leonidas had threatened Daisy with lawyers, had been neither forgiven nor forgotten.

But Leonidas was even more discomfited, ten minutes later, when, upstairs in Bain's apartment, Daisy announced she was entirely packed.

"That's it?" Leonidas looked with dismay at her two suitcases and a large cardboard box full of books and a single canvas painting. "That is everything you own?"

Daisy shrugged. "I sold most of our family's belongings last year, to pay for my father's legal defense." She hesitated as she said quietly, "The rest was sold to pay for the funeral."

Her eyes met his, and his cheeks burned. Though she didn't say more, he imagined her silently blaming him. When would she realize it wasn't his fault? Not his fault that her father had decided to sell forgeries and needed a lawyer. Not his fault that Patrick Cassidy had died of a stroke in prison!

But arguing wouldn't help anything. Choking back a sharp retort, he tried to imagine her feelings.

He took a deep breath.

"I'm sorry," he said slowly. "That must have been very hard."

Looking down, she whispered, "It was."

Leonidas glanced at the painted canvas resting in the cardboard box. It was a messy swirl of colors and shapes that seemed to have no unifying theme.

Following his glance, Daisy winced. "I know it's not very good."

Reaching down to the cardboard box, he picked up the painting. "I wouldn't say that…"

"Stop. I know it's terrible. I did it my final semester of art school. All I wanted was for it to be spectacular, amazing, so I kept redoing it, asking advice and redoing it based on everyone's advice. I wanted it to be as good as the masters."

"Maybe that's the problem. It looks like a mash-up of every well-known contemporary artist. What about your own voice? What were you trying to say?"

"I don't know," she said in a low voice. "I don't think I have a voice."

"That's not true," he said softly, looking at her bowed head. He thought of her years of love and loyalty. "I think you do."

Looking up, she gave an awkward laugh. "It's okay. Really. I tried to be an artist and failed. I never sold a single painting, no matter how hard I tried. So I threw them all away, except this one. I keep thinking," she said wistfully, brushing that canvas with her fingertips, "maybe someday, I'll figure it out. Maybe someday, I'll be brave enough to try again." She gave him a small smile. "Stupid, huh?"

Before he could answer, their driver knocked on the door. He'd come upstairs to help carry the suitcases. Leonidas lifted the big cardboard box in his arms. But he noticed Daisy continued to grip the painting in her hands. She carefully tucked it on top of everything else, so it wouldn't get crushed in the back of the Range Rover.

"Do you mind if we stop at the diner before we go back?" she said into the silence. He turned to her.

"Sure."

Her lovely face looked a little sad. "I think I need to talk to my boss."

They arrived at the cheerful, crowded diner, with its big windows overlooking vintage booths with Naugahyde seats. Jenkins pulled the SUV into the loading zone directly in front of the diner.

"Do you want me to come with you?" Leonidas asked.

"No," Daisy said.

Leonidas watched as she disappeared into the busy, bright diner. He thought of the morning they'd first met. She'd taken one look at his expensive designer suit and laughed. "Nice suit. Headed to court? Unpaid parking tickets?" With a warm smile, she'd held up her coffee pot. "You poor guy. Coffee's on me."

They'd ended up spending the rest of the day

together. If it had been one of his typical dates, he would have taken Daisy to the most exclusive restaurant in Manhattan, then perhaps out dancing at a club, then a nightcap at his mansion. But he'd known it couldn't be a date, not when he couldn't even tell her his real name.

So they'd simply spent the afternoon walking around her neighborhood in Brooklyn, visiting quirky little shops she liked, walking down the street lined with red brick buildings, ending with the view of the East River, and the massive bridge sticking out against the sky. Daisy greeted people by name on the street, warmly, and their eyes always lit up when they saw her.

It had been a wild ride, one that would put the roller coasters at Coney Island to shame. She'd made him come alive in a way he'd never imagined. Joy and color and light had burst into his life that day, from the moment he'd met her in this diner. It had been like a vibrant summer after a long, frozen winter.

But it could never be like that again. He would never be Leo again. Daisy would never look at him with love in her eyes again.

No. They would be partners. He wouldn't, couldn't, ask for more. Not when he had nothing more to give in return.

Waiting in the back seat of the Range Rover, he tried to distract himself with his phone. He had ten million messages from board members and designers and marketing heads, all of them anxious about various things; he found it difficult to care. He was relieved when he finally heard the SUV's door open.

"Everything all right?" he asked.

"I quit." Daisy gave a wistful smile. "Claudia—that's my boss—said she didn't need me to give notice. Turns out my job sitting at the cash register was not actually that useful, but she couldn't fire a pregnant single mother." She paused. "But now that I've got a billionaire baby daddy..."

Leonidas smiled. "You told her about me?"

She paused, then looked away. "Not everything."

Silence fell as his driver took them out of Brooklyn, crossing back over the bridge into Manhattan.

Leonidas watched her, feeling strangely sad. He fought to push the emotion away. Work, he thought. Work could save them.

"So you haven't heard of Vertigris or Helios," he said finally. "What about Bandia?"

Still looking out the window, Daisy shook her head.

"It's a small luxury brand that does only maternity clothing and baby clothing. We could go there to look for your coat."

"Okay." Her voice was flat.

"Or Astrara. Have you heard of that?"

Daisy finally looked at him, her face annoyed. "Of course I've heard of Astrara. I don't live under a rock."

Finally, she'd actually heard of one of his brands. He was slightly mollified. He maybe should have started with Astrara, as famous as Gucci or Chanel. "Which do you prefer to visit first? Bandia? Astrara? One of the others?"

"Does it matter?"

"Of course it matters," he said. He waited.

Daisy sat back against the seat. "Bandia," she sighed. "It sounds like it has the most reasonable prices."

Leonidas was careful not to disabuse her of that notion as they arrived at the grand Fifth Avenue boutique. After pulling in front, the driver turned off the engine. Tourists passing on the sidewalk gawked at them.

"Even in Manhattan," she grumbled. "Everyone stares at you."

Hiding a smile, Leonidas turned to help Daisy out. "They're looking at you."

Biting her lip, she took his hand, but to his disappointment, dropped it as soon as she was out of the SUV. As they walked into the boutique, Bandia's shop assistants audibly gasped.

"Mr. Niarxos!"

"You honor us!"

"Sir! We are so happy to…"

He cut them off with a gesture toward Daisy:

"This is my—" *future wife...baby mama...lover...* "—dear friend, Miss Cassidy. She needs a new wardrobe. I trust you can help her find things to her taste."

"Wardrobe!" Daisy gasped. She immediately corrected, "I just need a coat."

The assistants turned huge, worshipful eyes to Daisy. "Welcome to Bandia!"

"Miss Cassidy, may I get you some sparkling water? Fruit?"

"This way, if you please, to the private dressing suite, madam."

Perfect, Leonidas thought in approval. Just as he'd expected. He'd send the CEO of Bandia a note and let her know he approved of staff training levels.

"Madam, what type of clothes do you prefer?" The store's manager hurried to pay her obeisance as well. "Our newest releases for the fall line? Or perhaps the latest for resort?"

Daisy stared at them like a deer in headlights. "I just...need a coat," she croaked.

"Bring everything and anything in her size," Leonidas answered. "So she can decide."

They were both led to the VIP dressing suite, which had its own private lounge, where Leonidas could sit on a white leather sofa and drink champagne, as salesgirls brought rack after rack of expensive, gorgeous clothing for Daisy to try on in the adjacent changing room behind a thick white velvet curtain.

"I don't need all these clothes," she grumbled to Leonidas. "Why should I try them on, when I don't need them?"

"Market research?"

"Fine," she sighed.

Reluctantly, she tried on outfit after expensive outfit. Each time she stepped in front of the mirrors in the lounge, the salesgirls joyfully exclaimed over her.

"You look good in everything!"

"Beautiful!" another sighed.

"I hope when I'm pregnant someday I'll look half as good as you!"

It was true, Leonidas thought. Daisy looked good in everything. As she stood in front of the mirrors in an elegant maternity pantsuit, he marveled at her chic beauty.

"Do you like it?" he called.

Glancing back at him, she shrugged. "It's all right."

"Just all right?"

"It's not very… comfortable."

He frowned. That wasn't something he ever worried about. *"Comfortable?"*

"I prefer my T-shirts and stretch pants," she said cheerfully.

"Keep looking."

Rolling her eyes a little, Daisy continued to try

on clothes for the next hour, as Leonidas sat on the leather sofa, sipping complimentary Vertigris champagne—one of Liontari's other brands, from a two-hundred-year-old vineyard in France. His company was nothing if not vertically integrated.

Every time she stepped out of the changing room, to stand in front of the large mirrors in the lounge, Leonidas asked hopefully, "Do you like it?"

Always, the shrug. "It's fine."

"Fine?" A thousand-dollar maternity tunic was fine?

"Not as good as my usual T-shirts. Which, by the way, you can buy three for ten dollars." She tilted her head. "Is this the kind of market research you were looking for?"

Leonidas felt disgruntled. He'd hoped to impress her. Obviously it wasn't working. The only thing that had made Daisy's eyes sparkle was when the salesgirls brought over baby outfits that matched the postpartum clothes, cooing, "This will be perfect after your little one is born!"

Then Daisy looked at the price tag. "Three hundred dollars? For a baby dress that will be covered in spit-up, and probably only worn twice before she outgrows it?" She'd shaken her head. "And it's kind of scratchy. I want my baby to be comfortable and cozy, too!" Then Daisy looked around with a frown. "Don't you have any winter coats?"

The salesgirls looked at each other sheepishly. "I'm sorry, Miss Cassidy," one said. "It's March. We cleared out all the winter clothes for our new spring line."

"It's still snowing, and you're selling bikinis," Daisy said, her voice full of good-humored regret.

"There might be a few coats on the sales rack," one salesgirl said hesitantly.

Daisy seemed overjoyed when one puffy white coat fit her—if anything, it was a little too big. "And it's cozy, too!" Then she saw the price, and her smile disappeared. "Too much!"

"It's fifty percent off," Leonidas pointed out irritably.

"Still too much," Daisy said, but she continued hugging the coat around her tightly, as if she never wanted to take it off.

"We'll take it," he told the sales staff.

"I can't possibly let you pay—"

"You won't let me buy a cheap coat, from my own company? To warm the mother of my child? Are you really so unkind?"

Daisy hugged the coat around her, then said in a small voice, "All right, I guess. Thank you." She looked at Leonidas. "Are you ready to go?"

Finally. He'd convinced her to let him buy *something*. But he'd wanted to buy her so much more. "Not quite." He looked at the salesgirls. "She needs a ball gown."

As the staff left the lounge to gather the

dresses, Daisy looked at him incredulously. "A ball gown? You can't be serious."

"I'm taking you to a party on Saturday."

She groaned. "A party?"

"It's for charity." He quirked an eyebrow. "A fundraiser for homeless children. Don't you want to come and make sure they get a healthy chunk of my ill-gotten fortune?"

"Fine," she sighed. A moment later, when the salesgirls rolled a large rack of maternity ball gowns into the lounge, she grabbed the closest one, which was a deep scarlet red. She went back into the private changing room to try it on.

Leonidas waited to see it, practically holding his breath.

But when Daisy pushed back the curtain a few moments later, she was dressed in her white shirt and black leggings. "I'm done."

"But the gown?"

"The gown is fine."

She wasn't going to let him see it, he realized. Disappointed, he said hastily, "You must need new lingerie for—"

Daisy snorted. "I'm *not* trying that on in front of you. Are you ready to go?"

"Aren't there any other things you want to try on? Anything at all?"

"Nope." She turned with a smile to the sales-girls, hugging them. "Thank you so much for your help, Davina, Laquelle, Mary. And Posey—good luck on law school!"

Trust Daisy to make friends, instead of picking out designer outfits. As they left Bandia, going outside to where the SUV waited, Leonidas helped Daisy—now wearing her new white coat—into the back seat, as Jenkins tucked the carefully wrapped red ball gown into the trunk.

Daisy's pink lips lifted mischievously. "I'm sorry I didn't love all the clothes."

"It's fine." But he felt irritated. If not Bandia, surely one of his other luxury brands would make her appreciate his multibillion-dollar global conglomerate! He turned to Jenkins. "Take us to Astrara."

But even the dazzling delights of the famous three-story boutique, as enormous as a luxury department store, seemed to leave her cold. Daisy made friends with the salesgirls, and marveled at the cost of the clothes, which she proclaimed were also "weird looking" and "scratchy."

After that, he took Daisy to a luxury beauty and skin-care boutique, which seemed to bore her. "I like the stuff from the drugstore," she informed him.

Finally, in desperation, he took them to a famous perfumery on Fifth Avenue, Loyavault.

As she walked through the aisles of luxury perfume, she seemed dazzled by the lovely colors and bright boxes and lush scents. She bent her head to smell one perfume in a pink bottle, and her green eyes lit up with a bright smile.

"Wow," she whispered.

Leonidas felt the same, just looking at her.

He took the bottle from her hand. "Floral, roses and white jasmine, with an earthy note of amber." They stood close, so close, almost touching. "I'll have them wrap it up for you."

She bit her lip. "I shouldn't."

"I missed your birthday," he said quietly. "Won't you let me get you a present?"

She exhaled, then slowly nodded.

"But after this, we're done shopping."

Giving in to the inevitable, he sighed.

Daisy wasn't impressed by luxury. Or his company. Or him. It hurt his pride, a little. In each store, Daisy had been treated as if she were the queen of England, visiting from Buckingham Palace. Each time, she blushed with confusion, but was soon chatting with the staff on a first-name basis. And before long, the employees seemed to forget the powerful Liontari CEO was even there.

The salesgirls treasured Daisy for herself. He wasn't the only one to see Daisy's bright warmth. She shone like a star.

What a corporate wife she would make!

"Shall we go for lunch?" he asked as they left Loyavault. Outside, the March sun had come out, and the air was blue and bright, as the spring snow started to melt like it had never existed. She looked at him with a skeptical eye.

"Let me guess. Some elegant Midtown restaurant, French and fancy?"

He hastily rethought his restaurant choice.

"There's a place just a block away. It's French, but not fancy. Strictly speaking, it's not precisely French, but Breton. Crepes."

"You mean like pancakes? Yum."

Thus encouraged, he said, "Shall we walk? Or ride?"

"Walk."

They strolled the long city block to the small hole-in-the-wall establishment, tucked into a side street, where it had existed for fifty years. He led her into the wood-paneled restaurant, rustic as a Breton farmhouse, with a crackling wood-burning fire.

Unlike the more elegant restaurants, no one knew Leonidas here. He'd been here only once before, when he'd visited the city on a weekend from Princeton. They had to wait for a table.

But Daisy didn't seem to mind. She took his arm as they waited together in the tight reception space, and all of Leonidas's ideas of trying to bribe someone for an earlier table flew out the window.

Soon, a wizened host with a white beard led them to a tiny table for two near the fire. He didn't give them menus.

"You want the full?" the elderly man asked in an accented, raspy voice.

Leonidas and Daisy looked at each other.

"Yes?" he said.

"Sure?" she said.

"Cider," the man demanded.

"Just water," Leonidas replied. "Thank you."

After the waiter departed, he looked at Daisy across the table. "You don't really seem to like luxury. Fancy restaurants, fancy cars, fancy clothes."

She suddenly looked guilty. "I'm sorry. I don't mean to be rude…"

"You're never rude," he said. "I'm just curious why?"

"More market research?"

"If you like."

She sighed. "It all just seems so expensive. So…*unnecessary*."

"Unnecessary?" He felt a little stung. "Would you call *art* necessary?"

Daisy looked at him with startled eyes. "Of course it's necessary! It's an expression of the soul. The exploration and explanation of what makes us human."

"The same could be said of clothing. Or makeup or perfume. Or food."

She started to argue, then paused, stroking her chin.

"You're right," she admitted.

Leonidas felt a surge of triumph way out of proportion for such a small victory.

"Here," the white-bearded man said abruptly, shoving plates at them with savory buckwheat galettes, filled with the traditional ham, cheese and a whole cooked egg in the middle.

"Thank you." Daisy's eyes were huge. Then she took a bite. The sound of her soft moan of pleasure shook Leonidas. "It's—so—good," she breathed, and holding her fork like a weapon, she gobbled down the large crepe faster than he'd ever seen anyone eat before. He looked at her, and could think of nothing else but wanting to hear her make that sound again.

"Would you like another?"

"Another?" She licked her lips, and he had to grip the table.

"Save room for—dessert—" He managed to croak out. If only the dessert could be in his bedroom, with her naked, like that time with the ice cream. That would be the perfect end to their meal. Or anytime. Forever—

"Are you going to eat that?" Daisy said, looking longingly at his untouched crepe.

He pushed it toward her. "Please take it."

"Thank you," she almost sang, as if he'd just done something worthy of the Nobel Prize. And she ate that one, too, in rapid time.

Leonidas couldn't tear his eyes away as she lifted the fork to her mouth, before sliding it out again. As she leaned forward, her collar gaped, and he saw the push of her soft breasts against the hard wood of the table—

With a gulp, he looked away. A moment later, the plates were cleared.

"Ready for dessert?" the elderly man barked.

"Yes, please," she said, smiling back at him warmly. "I've never tasted anything so delicious in my life."

The old man frowned, and then his wrinkled eyes suddenly beamed at her. "You have good sense, madame."

Another conquest fell at Daisy's feet. But then, who could resist her?

Not Leonidas.

But he was, stupidly, the only man on earth who'd given his word of honor never to kiss her.

How strange it was, he thought. To want a woman like this, but not be able to touch her, not be able to seduce her. He thought he might literally die if he never possessed her again.

He would win her, he told himself fiercely. He would. And not just for one night, but forever.

"This is so good," Daisy moaned softly over the sweet crepe, drizzled with butter and sugar. Automatically pushing his own dessert crepe toward her, he tried to distract himself from his unbearable desire.

"I'm sorry you didn't care much for the shopping today."

"I liked the *people*... They were very nice."

"Some other day I'll show you more of Liontari's brands. I want you to appreciate my company. It will all belong to our child one day."

Daisy's eyes almost popped out of her head. She actually put down her fork. "Our daughter will inherit your company?"

Hadn't she realized that? Incredible. With any other woman, he thought, his business empire would have been the first thing on her mind. "Of course. It will all be hers."

Her forehead furrowed. "But what if...she doesn't want it?"

Now Leonidas was the one to be shocked. "Not want Liontari? Why would she not want it?"

Daisy took another bite, slowly pulling her fork out of her mouth, leaving a bit of sugar on her lower lip. He was distracted, until she said thoughtfully, "Not every child wants to follow in the footsteps of her parents' professions."

He looked up, annoyed. "It's not just a *profession*. It's a multibillion-dollar conglomerate, with the biggest luxury brands in the world—" He steadied himself, took a deep breath. Daisy couldn't have meant her words as an insult. "Don't worry." He made his voice jovial, reassuring. "I will teach her everything she needs to know. When it's her time to lead, she'll have the board members eating out of the palm of her hand."

"Yes. Maybe. If she wants."

"If she wants?" Leonidas repeated incredulously. "Why would anyone not want an empire?" Especially one he'd created out of his own sweat, blood and bone!

Daisy shrugged. "She might find running a corporation boring. Maybe she'll want to be… I don't know…an accountant. An actress. A firefighter!"

He was offering everything he had, everything he'd spent his life pursuing—everything that proved to the world, proved to himself, that his parents had been wrong, and Leonidas Niarxos had value, had a right to be alive.

But Daisy, who had such warmth and concern for strangers, didn't think his empire was worth anything? He thought their daughter might not want it?

He stared at her. "Are you serious?"

"I just want her to find her true passion. Like you found yours."

"My passion?"

"Isn't it obvious?" She gave him a cheeky smile. "Business is your passion."

Her smile did crazy things to his insides. "Business is my passion?"

"The way you've done it—yes. What else would you call it? There's no guidebook for creating a world empire. No business degree could tell a person how to do it."

"What's your passion, then?" he countered.

Her face fell, and she looked down at her plate. "Art, I guess. Even though I'm not very good at it."

She looked sad. He thought again about how she'd treasured that old painting.

Leonidas wanted to reassure her, but he didn't know how. At work, his leadership style was based on giving criticism, not reassurance.

As they left the restaurant, he thought about her words. *Business is your passion.* If that were true, why was it that for the last six months, he'd just been going through the motions at Liontari? He hardly cared about it at all anymore. He had yet to drag himself into the New York office, and the last few months in Paris, he'd barely bothered to criticize his employees.

As they walked out to where their driver waited with the Range Rover, Daisy suddenly nestled against him, wrapping her arm around his.

"Thank you," she whispered, and he felt her lips brush against the flesh of his ear. "For the crepes. The coat. The perfume." Pulling back, she looked at him, her eyes sparkling in the spring sun. "Thank you for a wonderful day."

He looked down at her, his heart pounding at the intimacy of her simple touch.

And suddenly, Leonidas couldn't imagine any passion, any longing, any desire greater than the one he had for her.

CHAPTER SIX

DAISY STARED AT herself in the mirror of her pretty cream-and-pink guest suite in Leonidas's New York mansion.

A stranger looked back at her, a glamorous woman in a red gown straight out of *Pretty Woman*. The dress caressed her baby bump, showcasing her full breasts, with a slit up the side of the skirt that showed off her legs. Long honey-brown hair hung thickly over her bare shoulders. Her eyelashes were darkened with mascara, her lips as red as the dress, all bought from the drugstore a few months ago. But she was wearing the scent Leonidas had bought her on their shopping excursion three days earlier. Even the shoes on her feet were new. That morning, just as she'd realized she could not possibly wear her scuffed-up black pumps with this dress, new shoes had mysteriously appeared at her door—strappy sandals covered with crystals in her exact size.

"Who are you?" Daisy said to the woman in the

mirror. Her voice echoed against the bedroom's high ceilings and white bed.

From the dog bed by the elegant fireplace, Sunny lifted her head in confusion. With a sigh, Daisy said to her, "It's all right, Sunny. I'm all right."

But was she?

She glanced back at her cell phone sitting on the vanity table, feeling dizzy. She didn't just look different now. She *was* different.

When she'd come out of the shower an hour before, she'd anxiously checked her online bank account to see if her most recent payment, a deposit for nursing school, had cleared yet. Once that money disappeared from her account, she expected to have very little left, so she was nervous about checks bouncing if she'd forgotten anything.

But looking at her bank account, she'd lost her breath. She'd closed her eyes and counted to five. Then she'd looked at her account again.

Her bank account had the scant hundreds she'd expected—*plus an extra million dollars*.

Leonidas had just made her a rich woman.

Why? How could he? She'd never asked for his money! Daisy shivered in the red dress. But she knew it wasn't for her, not exactly. It was to protect their baby, so she'd never worry or be afraid.

I will always provide for you. It's my job as a man. You would not try to deny me that.

Especially since she'd denied him other things. Like kisses. When, her first night here, he'd almost kissed her outside her bedroom door, she'd been far too tempted. It had scared her. She'd known, if she ever let him kiss her, that she would surrender everything.

And her life had already become unrecognizable enough. She looked at herself in the ball gown. Could she really keep his money—even for her baby?

It was true she'd already quit her job. When she'd gone to the diner, her boss had been all too happy for Daisy to leave her job, no advance notice required.

"We don't actually need an employee sitting at the register," Claudia had confided. "But I knew it hurt your feet to wait tables, and I couldn't fire you." She'd glanced at the Range Rover through the window. "But look at you now! It's a fairy tale! You said this Greek billionaire even wants to marry you?"

Daisy had winced. "I haven't agreed."

"Are you crazy?" Claudia gazed reverently at the handsome dark-haired tycoon, typing on his phone in the back seat. Then she frowned. "Have you told Franck?"

"I don't know why Franck would care." Daisy had smiled weakly. "I'm sure he'll just be glad to get me out of his apartment."

"You know he's in love with you."

Daisy rolled her eyes. "He was my father's best friend. He's not in love with me."

Claudia lifted an eyebrow. "Isn't he?"

She'd thought of his strange awkwardness when the middle-aged artist had proposed to her. *Stay as long as you want. Stay forever.*

And now, as Daisy looked in the mirror at the glamorous stranger in the red dress and red lipstick, she felt guilty that she hadn't told Franck she'd moved out and was now living with her baby's father. She didn't look forward to confessing Leonidas's name. Daisy hadn't even shared *that* with Claudia. Her bohemian friends had been her father's friends, too; they hated billionaires in general, but Leonidas Niarxos in particular, after he'd put her father in prison.

They would be horrified if they found out Daisy was having his baby. And if she ever became Leonidas's wife...

She took a deep breath. She didn't want to imagine it. Bad enough that tonight she'd be facing all of Leonidas's friends at a charity ball. They'd probably feel the same scorn for Daisy. They'd ask themselves what on earth the billionaire playboy saw in her. They'd think Leonidas was slumming with a waitress. Worse. Sleeping with the daughter of the convicted felon he'd put in prison.

Swallowing hard, Daisy looked at herself one last time in the mirror. Steadying herself on her high-heeled sandals, she lifted her chin, straightened her spine, and went downstairs.

Leonidas stood waiting at the bottom of the wide stone staircase. Her heart twisted when she saw him, darkly powerful and wide shouldered in a sleek black tuxedo. Their eyes locked.

"You look beautiful," he said in a low voice as she reached the bottom of the stairs. He visibly swallowed. "And *that dress*."

She gave him a shy smile. "You like it?"

Leaning forward, he whispered huskily, "You make me want to stay home tonight."

She shivered as he touched her, wrapping her faux fur stole around her bare shoulders. Taking his arm, she went out with him into the cold spring night, where Jenkins waited with the Rolls-Royce at the curb.

"Sorry," Leonidas said with a grin. "For tonight, a limo is required."

When they arrived at a grand hotel in Midtown Manhattan, Daisy was alarmed to see a red carpet set up at the entrance, where paparazzi waited, snapping pictures of the arriving glitterati. She turned accusingly on Leonidas. "You didn't say the charity ball was this big of a deal!"

"Didn't I?" His cruel, sensual lips curved upward. "Well. It's all for homeless kids."

Daisy looked with dismay at all the wealthy people walking the red carpet with photographers snapping. "I'll stick out like a sore thumb!"

"Yes." Leonidas looked at her in the back of limo, his black eyes gleaming as his gaze lingered on her red lips and red dress. "You're the most beautiful of them all."

As their driver opened the door, Leonidas stepped out, then reached back to her. "Shall we?"

Nervously, she took his hand. As they walked the red carpet, she clung to his muscled arm, trying to focus just on him, ignoring the shouts and pictures flashing.

"Leonidas Niarxos—is that your girlfriend?"

"Is she pregnant with your baby?"

He didn't answer, just kept looking down at Daisy with a soothing smile. For a moment she relaxed, lost in his dark eyes. Then she heard one of the paparazzi gasp.

"Oh, my God! That's the Cassidy kid! The daughter of the art forger who tried to swindle him!"

At that, there was a rush of questions. She quickened her step and didn't take a full breath until they were safely inside the hotel ballroom.

"How—how did they know who I was?" she choked out.

"They were bound to figure it out." Leonidas's dark eyes looked down at her calmly. "It's better this way."

"How can you say that?"

"There was always going to be some kind of scandal about us. Better for it to happen now, rather than later, after our daughter is born." He put his hand gently on her belly. "That way, it will only affect us. Not her."

It was the first time Leonidas had touched her belly. Even over the red fabric, she felt his gentle, powerful touch, felt his strength and how he wanted to protect them both.

It was strangely erotic.

"Are you ready?" he asked.

Holding her breath, she nodded. His dark eyes crinkled as he took her hand and led her through the double doors.

The hotel's grand ballroom was enormous, far larger than the one in his house, which now seemed quite modest by comparison. A full orchestra played big band hits from the nineteen forties as beautiful women in ball gowns danced with handsome men in tuxedos. On the edges of the dance floor, large round tables filled the space, each with an elaborate arrangement of white and red roses. Crystal chandeliers sparkled overhead.

Leonidas took two flutes of sparkling water from a waiter's silver tray. He handed her one of them, then nodded toward the far wall, his dark eyes gleaming. "Over there are the items that will be up for bidding in the auction tonight. Would you like to go see them?"

"Sure." Anything to give her something to do. To make her feel less out of place. People were staring at her, and she had no idea whether that was because her dress looked strange, or because they'd heard she was the art forger's daughter, or just because she wasn't beautiful enough to be on Leonidas's arm. She knew she wasn't, fancy ball gown or no. He was a handsome Greek billionaire. Who was she?

An ex-waitress. The daughter of a felon. A failed artist. Pregnant and unwed.

Nervously sipping the sparkling water, Daisy followed Leonidas to the long table lining the far wall of the hotel ballroom. Walking past all the items put forward in the upcoming charity auction, she stared at them each incredulously.

There was a guitar that had apparently once belonged to Johnny Cash. A signed first edition of a James Bond novel. Two-carat vintage diamond earrings. A small sculpture by a famous artist. And if the items weren't enough to whet the appetite, there were experiences offered on small illustrated posters: a week at someone's fully staffed vacation house in the Maldives. An invitation to attend Park City Film Festival screenings as the guest of a well-known actor. A dinner prepared at your home, for you and twelve of your best friends by a world-famous chef, who would fly in from his three-Michelin-star Copenhagen restaurant expressly for the occasion.

Walking past all the items, each more insane and over-the-top than the last, Daisy shook her head. Rich people really did live a life she could not imagine.

But on the other hand, it was all for charity, and if it really helped homeless kids…

She nearly bumped into Leonidas, who'd stopped at the end of the final table, in front of the very last item.

"Hey." She frowned up at him. "You nearly made me spill my—"

He glanced significantly toward that last item, his dark eyebrows raised. She followed his glance.

Then her hand clutched her drink. She felt like she was going to faint.

"That's—that's my—"

"Yes," he said. "It's your painting."

It was. Her final project from art school, in all its pathetic mess. Sitting next to all those amazing items that rich people might actually want.

Daisy looked around wildly. The noise and music and colors of the ballroom seemed to spin around her. She felt like she was in one of those awful dreams where you were in the hallway of your school and everyone was standing around you, laughing and pointing, and you suddenly realized you'd forgotten your homework—and your clothes.

She looked up at Leonidas with stricken eyes. "What have you *done*?"

He looked back at her. "Given you another chance."

"A chance at what!" she gasped. "Humiliation and pain?"

"A chance to believe in your dream," he said quietly. "I believe in you."

Shaking, Daisy wiped her eyes. She wanted to grab the painting and run, before any of these glamorous people could sneer at it.

But too late. She stiffened as two well-dressed guests came up behind them.

"What is this?" said the woman, who was very thin and draped in diamonds. "It's not signed."

Her escort peered doubtfully at the painting's description. "It says here that the artist wishes to be anonymous."

"How very strange." The woman turned to call to another friend, "Nan. Come tell me if you can guess who this artist is."

Daisy's cheeks felt like they were on fire, and her heart was beating fast, as if she'd just run two miles without stopping. Leonidas took her arm, and gently led her away from the auction table.

"It's to earn money for the charity. For the kids."

"It won't earn anything. No one will bid on it," she whispered. Why did he want to hurt her like this? She knew Leonidas didn't love her. But did he outright hate her? What other reason could he have to humiliate her, in front of all his ritzy friends?

She felt like she'd been ambushed, just when

she'd started to trust him. Leonidas believed in her? How could he, when she didn't believe in herself?

Later, after they sat down at their table for an elegant dinner of salmon in sauce, roasted fingerling potatoes and fresh spring vegetables, Daisy could hardly eat. She barely said a word to the guests sitting around them, in spite of their obvious curiosity about her. She let Leonidas speak for them. Yes, she was his date. Her name was Daisy. They were good friends. He was proud to say they were expecting a child together in June.

And all the while, Daisy was wondering how he could have done this to her.

During the days she'd stayed at his house, he'd gone out of his way to be kind to her. Leonidas Niarxos, the supposedly ruthless tycoon, had spent almost no time at work, other than the day he'd taken her shopping at Liontari's luxury boutiques. Instead, he'd kept her company doing the activities she enjoyed, like walking the dog, watching movies on TV and playing board games. Leonidas had listened patiently for hours as she'd read aloud from her pregnancy book, especially the section titled "How To Be an Expectant Father." She'd started to think he cared. She'd started to think he actually…liked her.

So why was he trying to hurt her like this?

"Cheer up," Leonidas whispered, as dinner

ended and they rose to go out on the dance floor. "The auction will be fun."

"Easy for you to say." Daisy tried not to feel anything as he pulled her into his arms. He was so powerful, so impossibly desirable in his sleek tuxedo. As he swayed her to the music, an old romantic ballad from the forties, he was the most handsome man in the world. Damn him.

He smiled down at her, his dark eyes twinkling. "Everything will be fine. I promise."

"Yes, it will," she retorted. "Because I'm leaving before the auction starts."

His smile dropped. "No. Please stay." Licking his lips, he added, "For the kids."

"For the kids," she grumbled. But it was strange. He didn't *seem* like a man bent on her destruction. Was it possible Leonidas wasn't actively trying to wreck her, but honestly believed someone might bid for her awful painting—against all those other amazing auction items?

If he did, he was deluding himself. Just like Daisy had, for years. In spite of getting mediocre marks in art school, she'd always hoped that somehow she might succeed and make a living from art, as her father had. That she'd find her voice, as Leonidas once said.

But she never had. Instead, she'd spent years suffering that terrible hope, getting gallery shows in Brooklyn, Queens and Staten Island through her father's connections, only to sell nothing.

Friends *had* offered to come to the shows and buy her paintings, but of course Daisy couldn't allow that. Her friends didn't have money to waste, and anyway, she would have been glad to paint them something for free.

But none of her friends had asked for a free painting. Which could mean only one thing: even her friends didn't like her art, not really.

Even Daisy herself wasn't sure about it. But she'd still tried to force herself to be upbeat, desperately trying to promote her art to bored strangers.

A year of that. Of awful hope, and finally crushing despair. There had been only one good thing to come from her father's trial—a horrible silver lining that she'd never admitted, even to herself. He had needed her, and that had given her an excuse to surrender the horror of her dream.

But now, Daisy was being forced to relive it all. She would never forgive Leonidas for this.

"Are—you—ready?" The auctioneer chanted from the stage. There was an excited hubbub from guests at the cleared tables. Women in ball gowns and men in tuxedos sat on the edge of their seats, ready to bid vast fortunes for amusements and whims. *For the kids,* Daisy repeated to herself.

Leonidas put his arm around her. "Try to enjoy this," he whispered. Daisy stared at the oversize arrangement of white and red roses on the table and tried to breathe. Soon this would all be over.

"Let's get started," the auctioneer boomed into the microphone. "For our first item…"

Everything sold quickly—the guitar, the autographed book, the week in the Maldives. The audience was full of smiles and glee, happily getting into bidding wars with their friends, as if they were bidding with counterfeit money, and no amount was too high.

And finally…

"For our last item, we have an unsigned painting, by Anonymous. Do I have a bid?" Even the auctioneer sounded doubtful. "Uh, let's start the bidding at…two hundred dollars."

It was the lowest starting bid of the night, by far. And Daisy knew that no one would even want to give that much. She braced herself for a long, awkward silence, after which Leonidas would be forced to make a pity bid, to try to save face. He would see he had no reason to believe in her. Even *he* would be forced to admit that Daisy was a talentless hack. She was near tears.

"Two hundred dollars," someone called from the back.

Who was it? Daisy blinked, craning her neck.

"Three hundred," called a woman from a nearby table. She was a stranger. Daisy didn't know anyone here, except Leonidas.

"Five hundred," someone else said.

"A thousand," cried an elderly man from the front.

The bidding accelerated, became hotly contested— even more than the guitar once owned by Johnny Cash. Daisy sat in shock as the number climbed.

Five thousand. *Ten.* Twenty. Fifty thousand. *A hundred thousand dollars.*

Daisy was hyperventilating. Through it all, Leonidas kept silent.

Until…

"One million dollars." His deep, booming voice spoke from beside her. Sucking in her breath, she looked up at him. He smiled back, his dark eyes warm.

"Sold! To the gentleman at table thirteen!"

As people at their table clustered around him, shaking his hand and congratulating him on the winning bid, Daisy trembled with emotion. She couldn't believe what had just happened.

I believe in you.

But it hadn't just been Leonidas who'd bid for her painting. He hadn't said a word, not until the end. Other people had bid for it. A bunch of strangers who had no idea Daisy was the artist. She hadn't had to beg them to buy it. They'd all just wanted it.

Was it possible she'd been wrong, and she did have some talent after all…?

Leonidas turned away from his friends. He

looked down at her, his dark gaze glittering. "They'll deliver the painting later. Do you want to leave?"

Wordlessly, Daisy nodded.

Outside, the Manhattan street was dark and quiet, except for the patter of cold rain. As they hurried toward the limo waiting in a side lane near the hotel, the rain felt like ice against her skin. Leaning over her, Leonidas tried to protect Daisy from the weather with his arms, with only a small amount of success. They were both laughing as they slid damply into the back seat of the Rolls-Royce.

"Take us home," Leonidas told Jenkins, who nodded and turned the wheel.

"Home," Daisy echoed, and in that moment, the brownstone mansion almost did feel like home. For a moment, they smiled at each other.

Then the air between them electrified.

She abruptly turned away, toward the window, where the lights of the city reflected in the puddles of rain. She felt Leonidas's gaze on her, but she couldn't look at him. Emotions were pounding through her like waves.

Once they arrived at his mansion, she followed him up the steps to the entrance. He punched in the security code, and they entered, to find it dark and quiet.

"Everyone must have gone to bed." He gave a low laugh. "Even your dog must be asleep, since she's not rushing to greet us." He flicked on the foyer's light, causing the crystal chandelier to illuminate in a thousand fires overhead, reflecting on the stately stone staircase behind them.

Taking her fur stole, Leonidas hung it in the closet. He looked down at Daisy, who was still silent. His handsome face became troubled.

"Daisy, did I do wrong?" He set his jaw. "If I did, I'm sorry. I thought if—"

"You believed in me, when I didn't believe in myself," she whispered.

His dark eyes met hers. "Of course I believe," he said simply. "I always have. From that first day at the diner, I saw you were more than beautiful. You're the best and kindest woman I've ever met—"

Reaching up, Daisy put her hands on his broad shoulders, feeling the fabric of his tuxedo jacket, damp with rain. And lifting her lips to his, she kissed him passionately.

A moment before, entering the house, Leonidas had looked at Daisy's lovely, distant face as she'd stood half in shadow. For the first time, he'd questioned whether he'd done the right thing, offering her painting at the charity fundraiser without her knowledge or permission.

But the idea of Daisy giving up her dreams was unbearable to Leonidas. Whether her painting was actually worth a million dollars, or a hundred, he didn't care. He was accustomed to his own despair, but a world where a warm, loving woman like Daisy had no hope was a world he did not want to live in.

So he'd taken the painting from the guest room, and offered it to the charity's auction committee. He'd known if the painting was the last item up for auction, that at least a few people in the audience, after imbibing champagne all night, would assume the painting was an unknown masterpiece, and that others, seeing the bidding war heat up, would not want to be left out, and would swiftly follow suit.

Leonidas would never forget the look on Daisy's beautiful face when her student painting had sold for a million dollars. Not until the day he died.

As they'd left the grand hotel, he'd gloried in the successful outcome of his plan. But she'd been silent all the way home, refusing to meet his eyes. He'd started to have doubts. Perhaps he should have asked her permission. Perhaps—

And so he'd turned to her, as they stood alone at the base of the stone staircase. But even as he'd tried to ask, he'd been unable to look away from her.

Daisy was more beautiful than any art ever created.

Her long brown hair fell over her bare shoulders. Her full breasts thrust up against the low sweetheart neckline of her red column dress, the fabric falling gently over the swell of her pregnant belly. Her dark lashes fluttered against her cheek as her teeth worried against her lower lip, so plump and red.

In the shadows of the foyer, the sparkling light refracted in the hundred-year-old crystal chandelier, gleaming against her lips, her cheekbones, her luminous eyes.

And then she'd kissed him.

As her soft lips touched his, he felt a shock of electricity that coursed down his body, from his hair to his fingertips to his toes. His muscles went rigid. He burned, then melted.

He'd been forcing himself to abide by his promise not to touch her. But every day, every hour, he'd felt the agony of that. All he'd wanted to do was kiss her, seduce her, possess her.

But now she was kissing *him*.

With a rush, he cupped his hands along her jawline, moving back to tangle in her hair, drawing her close. He kissed her hungrily, twining his tongue with hers. He felt out of control, as if his hunger might devour them both. He wrenched away, looking down at her. His heart was pounding.

"Come to bed with me," he whispered, running his hand down her throat, along the bare edge of her collarbone. He felt her tremble. Lowering his head, he softly kissed her throat, running his hand through her hair. "Come to bed…"

Her green eyes were reckless and wild. Wordlessly, she nodded. But as he took her hand to lead her to the stairs, she swayed and seemed to stagger, as if her knees had gone weak.

With one swoop, Leonidas lifted her up into his arms. She weighed nothing at all, he thought in wonder. As he carried her up the carved stone staircase, he looked down at her, marveling that she had such power over him.

She'd bewitched him, utterly and completely. As he carried her up the stairs, all the darkness of his world receded. When he looked into her eyes, his heart felt warm and alive, instead of frozen in ice. Beneath the soft glow of her eyes, he could almost believe he wasn't the monster his parents had believed him to be. Maybe he was someone worthy. Someone good.

Leonidas carried her down the hall, into his shadowy bedroom, lit by dappled lights from the window. Outside, the city had fallen into deepening night. Across the street, he could see the illuminated tips of skyscrapers peeking over the rooftops, and beyond that, the twinkling stars, cold and distant.

He lowered her reverently to the king-sized bed. Her honey-brown hair swirled like a cirrus cloud across the pillows. She looked up at him with heavy-lidded eyes, and he caught his breath.

Leonidas dropped his tuxedo jacket and tie to the floor. Kicking off his shoes, he fell next to her on the bed. He slowly removed each of her high-heeled sandals, first one, then the other. Leaning forward, he cupped her face and kissed her tenderly. Her lips parted as he felt her sigh, and it took every ounce of his willpower to hold himself back, when all he wanted to do was possess her. *Now*.

But he held himself back. She was pregnant with his baby. He would not overwhelm her. He would be gentle. He'd take his time. Lure her. *Seduce her*.

And make her his own—forever.

Reaching out, he gently cupped her cheek. His hand stroked whisper soft down her neck, to her bare shoulder.

With an intake of breath, she met his gaze. Her eyes were full of tears as she tried to smile.

"Leo," she whispered.

His heart lifted to his throat.

Leo. She'd called him Leo. The name she'd used long ago, before she knew his true identity, back when she'd loved him...

Leonidas shuddered with emotion. Wrapping his arms around her, he pulled her tight. As he kissed her, memories from last fall, when he'd known such joy in her arms, filled him body and soul. The night he'd first kissed her in Brooklyn, the night he'd taken her virginity, all the nights after.

But this kiss was even better.

Because now, Daisy knew who he was. She'd kissed him first. She knew the worst of him, but still wanted him.

Except she *didn't* know the worst. He sucked in his breath. And she must never know…

No. He must not think of it. Not now. Not ever.

He deepened the kiss, until it became rough, almost savage in his need to obliterate all else. Daisy's embrace was passionate and pure, like the woman herself. Being in her arms was the only thing that made him forget…

All thought, all reason, fled his mind as her lips seared his. Part of him almost expected she'd stop him, pull back, tell him she was too good for him—and how could he deny the truth of that?

But she did not pull away. Instead, her lips strained against his, matching his fire. The whole world seemed to whirl around him as he held her, facing each other on the bed. He kissed slowly down her throat.

"Sweet," he groaned against her skin. "So sweet."

Her hands reached for the buttons of his white shirt. When they wouldn't easily open, she reached beneath the fabric in her impatience, and stroked his bare chest. Sitting up, he ripped the shirt off his body, causing the final buttons to scatter noisily across the marble floor, along with his platinum cufflinks.

Turning back to her, he unzipped the back of

her red gown and gently pulled it down her body, revealing her white strapless bra, barely containing her overflowing breasts, and then her full, pregnant belly, her white lace panties clinging to her hips.

He tossed the ball gown to the floor. He almost could not bear to look at her, she was so beautiful, looking up at him in the tiny white lingerie that revealed her explosive curves, her brown hair glossy and coiled over the pillows, her green eyes dark with desire.

"Kiss me," she whispered.

A low groan escaped him, and he obeyed. He turned her to face him, kissing her for moments, or maybe for hours. Time seemed to stretch and compress as he was lost in her embrace. He kissed down her throat to the edge of the white satin bra. Reaching around her back, he loosened the clasp, and the fabric fell away. He looked at her breasts, so deliciously full, and holding his breath, he reached out to cup them with his hands.

Her lips parted and her eyes closed, her expression lost in pleasure. He stroked her full nipples, causing them to pebble beneath his touch. Lowering his head, he pulled one into his mouth, swirling it with his tongue, suckling her.

Her hands gripped the white duvet, as if she felt herself flying into the sky. He tenderly kissed around the curve of her full, pregnant belly. Mov-

ing back up, he kissed her lips long and linger-
ingly, before he finally drew back.

Cupping her cheek, he looked down at her with
sudden urgency in the darkness of the bedroom,
with the twinkling lights of Manhattan slanted
across the marble floor like trails of diamonds.

"Marry me," he whispered. "Marry me, Daisy."

CHAPTER SEVEN

MARRY HIM?

Daisy's eyes flew open. She was naked, melting beneath his touch. She wanted him; oh, how she wanted him.

But marry him?

"I…" She shivered as Leonidas slowly stroked his warm hand down her cheek to her throat and the crevice between her breasts. Every part of her ached for his touch. Not just her body. Her heart.

Looking at him in the shadowy bedroom, she'd suddenly seen the man she'd loved last fall. Leo. Her Leo. Her lover, with whom she'd spent so many days laughing, talking, kissing in the sunlight, holding hands beneath the autumn leaves. He hadn't taken her virginity. She'd given it to him. Her Leo.

But could she surrender everything? Could she ever forgive herself if she did? What kind of woman would she be?

"I can't marry you," she whispered.

"You know me." His hands stroked softly down

her body. Closing his eyes, he rested his head in the valley between her breasts. Surprised, she looked down and placed her hands gently against his dark hair. "I want to be with you. Always."

That couldn't be tears in his eyes. No, impossible. Leonidas Niarxos was ruthless. He had no heart. He himself had said so.

And yet, somehow Leonidas had become her Leo again. His eyes were like pools of darkness glittering with stars, as deep and unfathomable as the night. His body was Leo's. His tanned, muscular chest was powerful, his skin like satin over steel. Daisy's fingers wonderingly stroked his rough dark hair, his small, hard nipples, then down over the flat muscles of his belly.

Leo, but not Leo. Not exactly. She knew too much now. *Leo* had been her equal. This man was more powerful than Daisy in every possible way. He was a famous, self-made billionaire who'd crushed the world beneath his Italian leather shoe, building a global fortune. He was the most eligible playboy in the world, handsome and rich, the man every woman wanted.

And yet—

And yet, in this moment, she saw a strange vulnerability in his black eyes. He watched her as if he expected, at any moment, she might break the spell, and break his heart.

It was an illusion, she told herself.

But as he lowered his mouth passionately to

hers, she was lost in his embrace as he wrapped his powerful arms around her. His lips plundered hers, his tongue teasing and tempting. His hands stroked down her body, cupping her full breasts, moving down her full belly to the curve of her hip.

Then his kiss gentled. He held her against his muscular chest as if she were a precious treasure. His hand cupped her cheek tenderly.

"Marry me," he whispered. "And I'll hold nothing back. I will give you everything."

Everything? What did he mean? "You already gave me too much. That money in my bank account—"

"I'm not talking about money."

Then what? Her heart lifted to her throat. He couldn't mean—he might be able to truly love her?

Lowering his head, he kissed her. His sensual fingertips caressed her bare skin, from her shoulder, to the sensitive crook of her neck. He softly stroked the tender flesh of her earlobe, his fingers tangling in her long hair, as need sizzled through her.

He cupped her breast, rubbing his thumb against her nipple. Leaning forward, he drew her tight, aching nipple into the wet heat of his mouth. She gasped as she felt the hot swirl of his tongue suckling her, the roughness of his chin against her skin.

Pushing her legs apart, he knelt between her thighs on the bed. His broad-shouldered body was silhouetted by the city's dappled light outside. His black eyes gleamed as he slowly pulled her white lace panties down from her hips, like a whisper over her thighs, past her knees and calves, tossing them to the floor.

Shivering with desire, she closed her eyes, her head straining back against the pillows. He spread her thighs wide with his powerful hands, moving his head between her legs. He paused, and she felt the heat of his breath against her skin.

Then, finally, he lowered his head to taste her. His hot, sensual tongue swirled against her, lightly, delicately, then lapping with more force, pushing inside her as she gasped with pleasure. The delicious tension coiled inside her, building higher and higher, until, suddenly, she cried out with joy, rocked by ecstasy.

She was still gasping beneath waves of pleasure when he lifted himself up, holding himself over her belly with his powerful arms. Positioning himself between her legs, he pushed inside her with one deep thrust.

A hoarse groan escaped him as filled her, stretching her to the hilt. For a split second, it was too much.

Then, as he held himself still, allowing her body to adjust, incredibly, new pleasure began to build inside her. He thrust inside her again, slowly. But the muscles of his arms seemed to bulge and shake, and a bead of sweat formed on his forehead, from the effort of holding himself back.

Suddenly, he pulled back. Falling onto the bed beside her, he gently rolled her on top of him.

"Take me," he said huskily, his dark eyes like fire. "I'm yours, if you want me."

If she wanted him?

She wanted him—yes. But he'd never asked her to take control before. Feeling uncertain, she hesitated, her body suspended over his. He was so huge. Then, slowly, she positioned herself, lowering her body, pulling him inside her, inch by delicious inch. The pleasure was almost too much to bear.

Then she looked down at his face.

His expression was worshipful, almost holy, as if he held his breath, as if he were barely holding on to the shreds of self-control. Her confidence grew.

Slowly, she began to ride him. As she picked up rhythm, he gasped aloud, a single choked groan. He suddenly gripped her thighs with his large hands.

"Daisy—slow down—I can't—I can't—"

But she was merciless, driving forward. Pulling him inside her deeply, she increased her speed, going faster and faster. Her full breasts swayed as she rocked back and forth, sliding hot and wet against him, until, gripping her fingernails into his shoulders, she hit another sharp peak, even higher and more devastating than the one before, and she screamed.

He exploded, pouring himself into her with a guttural roar.

She collapsed forward against him, sweaty and spent. He cradled her gently into his arms, kissing her temple.

"Daisy—*agape mou*—"

It had been his old nickname for her, and at that, her heart finally could take no more.

How could she have ever thought she couldn't love him again? How could she have imagined she could ever protect her heart?

Daisy's eyes flew open in the darkness.

She was in love with him. She always had been, even in the depths of her hatred and hurt. She'd never stopped loving him.

Turning to face him on the bed, she looked at his handsome face beneath a beam of silvery moonlight pouring like rain through the window. She whispered, "Yes."

Leonidas grew very still. "Yes?"

Tears filled her eyes, tears Daisy didn't understand. Were they tears of grief—or joy?

Twining her fingers in his dark hair, she tried to believe it was joy.

"I'll marry you, Leo," she said.

* * *

They were wed four days later.

The ceremony was small and quiet, held in the ballroom of Leonidas's house—"Your house now," he'd told her with a shy smile. A home wedding was perfect. The last thing Daisy wanted was more attention.

After all the pictures paparazzi took of them together at the charity ball, the story that Leonidas Niarxos had impregnated the daughter of the man he'd put into prison had exploded across New York media. For a few days, photographers stalked their quiet West Village lane. Daisy felt almost like a prisoner, afraid to go outside.

Even after they'd decided to have the wedding ceremony at home, Daisy had nervously wondered how her friends would be able to get through the media barricades.

Then a miracle happened.

The day before their wedding, a scandal broke about a movie star having a secret family in New York, a longtime mistress and two children, while he also had a famous actress wife and four children at his mansion in Beverly Hills. The national scandal trumped a local one, and all the paparazzi and news crews and social media promoters left Leonidas and Daisy's street to stalk the movie star and his two beleaguered wives instead.

Daisy spent her last day before the ceremony finalizing the details with the wedding planner, who'd been provided by Liontari's PR department, and then going to a lawyer's office to sign a prenuptial agreement which, in her opinion, was far too generous. "I'm not looking to get more money," she'd protested to her fiancé. "You've already given me a million dollars."

"That money means nothing to me. I always want you and the baby to feel safe," Leonidas said.

"But the prenuptial agreement would give me millions more. It just doesn't seem fair."

"To who?"

"To you."

Smiling, he'd taken her in his arms. "I'm fine with it. Because I never intend for us to get divorced." Lowering his head to hers, he'd whispered, "You've made me so happy, Daisy…"

They spent the last night before their wedding in bed. Daisy never wanted him to let her go.

And now he never would.

On the morning of their wedding, as she got ready, Daisy was overjoyed to see the spring sun shining warmly, with almost no paparazzi left on the street to bother them.

She invited only about twenty friends to the ceremony. She'd been too cowardly to call Franck in California and tell him she was getting married. She'd decided to tell him after the honeymoon. She told herself she didn't want to have to refuse him, if he offered to walk her down the aisle in lieu of her father. No one could replace her father.

Daisy already felt disloyal enough, marrying the man who'd killed him.

No, she told herself. Leonidas didn't kill my father. He just accused him of forgery.

If only she could believe her father really had been guilty. Because if her father had knowingly tried to sell a forged painting, how could she blame Leonidas for refusing to be swindled?

But her father had sworn he was innocent. How could Daisy doubt his word, now that he was dead? Even now, she felt guilty, wondering if her father was spinning in his grave at her disloyalty.

She would walk down the aisle alone.

Coming down the stairs, Daisy paused in the quiet foyer before entering the ballroom. Giving a nervous smile to the hulking guards who stood by the mansion's front door, providing security for the event, she clutched her bouquet of lilies against her simple white silk shift dress. A diamond tiara glittered in her upswept hair, along with the huge diamond on her finger.

Everything for today's ceremony, including Leonidas's tuxedo, had been carefully chosen from Liontari's various luxury brands, ready to be pictured, packaged and posted by the official wedding photographer onto social media accounts, and released to newspapers around the world.

"You can't buy this kind of press," the PR woman had said, smacking her lips.

Daisy might have preferred something a little less fancy. But Leonidas had already given her so much. He'd barely gone to work all week. When he'd asked her if she minded if their wedding promoted Liontari brands, she'd wanted to help. She'd had only one prerequisite.

"As long as the dress is comfortable," she'd said. And it was, the white silk loose and light against her skin.

With a deep breath, Daisy opened the ballroom doors.

The bridal march played, and all the guests turned to look at her. As she came down the makeshift aisle between the chairs, her knees shook. She wished she'd taken Mrs. Berry's idea and let Sunny walk her down the aisle. But the dog was still so young, not fully trained, and liable to rush off and chase or sniff. She glanced at the dog, sitting in the front row, tucked carefully at the housekeeper's feet. Daisy gave a nervous smile, and the dog panted back happily, seeming to smile.

The emotions of the other guests were more complicated.

On one side of the aisle she saw her own friends, artists and artisans, in wacky, colorful clothes. On the other side sat Wall Street tycoons,

Park Avenue socialites and international jet-setters in sleek couture.

The only thing which both sides seemed to agree on was that Daisy was a greedy sellout, a gold digger cashing in, marrying the man who'd killed her father.

She stopped to catch her breath. No. She was just imagining that. No one would think that. She forced herself forward.

But as Daisy walked past the bewildered eyes of her friends, and the envious, suspicious faces of the glitterati, she felt very alone.

Then her eyes met Leonidas's, where he stood beside the judge at the end of the aisle. And she remembered all the joys of the last week. The sensuality. The laughter. The trust. They were going to be a family.

Gripping her bouquet, she came forward. The judge took a deep breath.

"My friends," the man intoned, "we are gathered here today…"

There was a hubbub at the door. Someone was hoarsely yelling, trying to push in. Daisy whirled to look.

A gray-haired man was trying to push into the ballroom, struggling against the two beefy security guards.

Franck Bain.

Daisy's lips parted. Why was he here? How had he found out?

"You can't marry him!" the middle-aged artist cried, his shrill voice echoing across the ballroom. "Don't do it, Daisy! I can take care of you!"

Leonidas made a gesture to two other guards hovering nearby, and they quickly moved to assist. The four security guards grabbed the thin man, who was struggling and panting for breath.

"Don't marry him!" Franck gasped. "He's a liar who killed your father—an innocent man!"

As he was forcibly pulled from the ballroom, the double doors closed with a bang.

A very uncomfortable silence fell.

"Shall I continue?" the judge said.

The guests looked at each other, then at the bridal couple. The PR team, who were filming the event live for Liontari's social media feeds, seemed beside themselves with delight at the unscripted drama.

Daisy's heart thundered in her chest. She wanted to fling away her bouquet, to make a run for it—run from all the judgment and guilt, her own most of all.

But her gaze fell on her engagement ring, sparkling on her hand, resting on her pregnant belly. Run away? That would truly be the act of a coward. No matter how much anyone criticized her for it, she'd already made her decision. She was bound to Leonidas, not just by their child, but by her word, freely given four days before.

I'll marry you, Leo.

Daisy met Leonidas's burning gaze, and she tried to smile. She nodded at the judge, who swiftly resumed the ceremony.

Ten minutes later, they were signing the marriage certificate. And just like that, they were wed.

Leonidas kissed her as the judge pronounced them husband and wife, but his kiss was oddly polite and formal. As they accepted the congratulations of their guests, Daisy's friends also seemed uncomfortable, their eyes sliding away awkwardly even as they pretended to smile.

At the wedding reception, held on the other side of the elegant ballroom, the very best champagne and liquor was served, all from Liontari's brands. The PR crew gleefully filmed all the glamorous, exotic guests, the wealthy and the beautiful and brightly bohemian, laughing and dancing and eating lobster, pretending to have the time of their lives.

But underneath it, Daisy felt hollow.

Don't marry him. He's a liar who killed your father—an innocent man.

The reception seemed to last forever. Leonidas was strangely distant, even though he was right beside her, and after hours of forced smiling, Daisy's face ached. Finally, the last guest drank the last flute of champagne, left the last gift, and departed. Even Mrs. Berry left, with Sunny in tow, leaving only the bridal couple and the PR team in the ballroom.

"You can go," Leonidas told them. The PR woman looked back brightly.

"I was thinking, Mr. Niarxos, we could come on your honeymoon, if you like, and get shots of you two kissing and frolicking on the beach—"

Beach? What beach? Daisy frowned. They hadn't planned a honeymoon. Did the woman imagine them at Coney Island or the Jersey shore? Only if "frolicking" meant shivering to death in the cool March weather!

"That kind of access would be invaluable," the PR woman chirped. "It would almost certainly go viral—"

"No," Leonidas said firmly. "No more filming."

Daisy went almost weak with gratitude as the PR team departed, leaving them alone at last.

Leonidas turned to Daisy.

"Mrs. Niarxos," he said quietly.

She swallowed. Her heart pounded as her husband pulled her closer. She felt his warmth and strength. She felt so right in her husband's arms. This marriage was right. It had to be right.

He lifted a dark eyebrow. "Did you know Bain was going to come here?"

She shook her head a little shamefacedly. "I'm sorry." She bit her lip, her cheeks hot. "I don't

know how he found out about the wedding. I
didn't tell him—"

"It's all right. I don't blame the man for wanting you."

"You—you don't?"

"Any man would," Leonidas whispered. Lowering his head, he kissed her tenderly. Then he
pulled back with a smile. "Our plane is waiting."

"Plane?"

Leonidas took a deep breath. "I told you, if you
agreed to marry me, I would hold nothing back.
I'm a man of my word."

*Marry me. And I'll hold nothing back. I will
give you everything.* When he'd said the words
to her, she'd hoped he meant his heart. "So that
means a honeymoon?"

He mumbled something. Frowning, she peered
up at him.

"What?"

He lifted his head. "I'm taking you to Greece.
To the island where I was born." He gave her a
crooked smile. "Mrs. Berry has already packed
your suitcase."

"What about Sunny?"

Leonidas smiled. "Mrs. Berry has promised
to give her the same love she gives her own Yor-
kies at home."

It was strange not to have Sunny with her,
as they left ten minutes later for an overnight
flight. After all the drama of the last few days

leading up to their wedding, once they were settled on the private jet, Daisy felt her exhaustion. She promptly fell asleep in her husband's arms and did not wake again until an hour before they landed on the small Greek island in the Aegean.

As they came down the steps from their private jet to the tarmac, Daisy looked around, blinking in the bright Greek sun. A burst of heat hit her skin.

It was already summer on this island. She was glad she'd taken a shower on the plane and dressed for the weather, in a white sundress and sandals. Her hair was freshly brushed and long, flowing over her bare shoulders. Even Leonidas was dressed casually—at least, casually for him—in a white shirt with the sleeves rolled up, top buttons undone, over black trousers.

To her surprise, no driver came to the small airport to collect them; instead, a vintage convertible was parked near their hangar, left by one of his staff members.

"Get in," Leonidas said with a lazy smile, as he tossed their suitcases in the back. He drove them away from the tiny airport, along the cliffside road.

Daisy's hair flew in the warm breeze of the convertible, as she looked around a seaside Greek village. She'd never seen anything so lovely as the picturesque white buildings, many covered with pink flowers and blue rooftops, with the turquoise sea and white sand beach beneath the cliffs.

Turning off the slender road, Leonidas pulled up to a gate and typed in a code. The gate swung open, and he drove through.

Daisy gasped when she saw a lavish white villa, spread out across the edge of the beach, overlooking the sea.

"This was your childhood home?" she breathed, turning to him. "You were the luckiest kid alive."

His eyes seemed guarded as he gave a tight smile. "It is very beautiful. Yes."

Parking in the separate ten-car garage, which was almost empty of cars, he turned off the engine. After taking their luggage from the trunk, he led Daisy inside the villa.

They were greeted by a tiny white-haired woman who exclaimed over Leonidas in Greek and cried and hugged him. After a few moments of this, he turned to Daisy.

"This is Maria, my old nanny. She's housekeeper here now."

"Hello," Daisy said warmly, holding out her hand. Maria looked confused, looking from Daisy's face to her belly. Then Leonidas spoke a few words in Greek that made the white-haired woman gasp. Ignoring Daisy's outstretched hand, the housekeeper hugged her, speaking rapidly in the same language.

"She's thrilled to meet my wife. She says it's about time I was wed," he said, smiling.

"Maria helped raise you?"

His expression sobered. "I don't know how I would have survived without her."

"Your parents weren't around?"

"That's one way to put it." He turned to Maria and said something in Greek.

The white-haired woman nodded, then called out, bringing two men into the room. They spoke to Leo and then took their suitcases down the hall.

Leonidas turned to Daisy. "You must be hungry."

"Well—yes," she admitted, rubbing her belly. "Always, these days." She bit her lip. "And I didn't eat much at the reception last night…"

"We can have lunch on the terrace. The best part of the house."

He led her through the spacious villa, which was elegant and well maintained, but oddly old-fashioned, almost desolate, like a museum. She asked, "How long has it been since you've visited?"

He glanced around the music room, with its high ceilings and grand piano, its wide windows and French doors overlooking the sea. He scratched his head. "A few years. Five?"

"You haven't been home for *five years*?"

"I was born here. I never said it was home." He

looked away. "I don't have many good memories of the place. I was away at school from when I was nine, remember. I've hardly come back since my parents died."

She knew he was an orphan. "I'm so sorry... how old were you?"

"Fourteen." His voice was flat. No wonder. It was heartbreaking to lose your parents. Daisy knew all about it.

Her voice was gentle as she said, "Why did you choose this place for our honeymoon?"

"Because..." He took a deep breath. "Because it was time. Besides." He gave a smile that didn't meet his eyes. "Doesn't every bride dream of a honeymoon on a Greek island?"

"It's more than I ever dreamed of." She nestled her hand in his. "I'm sorry about your parents. My own mom died when I was just seven. Cancer. And then my..."

She stopped herself, but too late. Their eyes locked. Would the memory of her father always stand between them?

He pulled his hand away. "This way."

Leonidas led her outside through the French doors. Daisy stopped, gasping at the beauty.

The wide terrace clung to the edge of the bright blue sea, with a white balustrade hovering between sea and sky. On the walls of the villa behind them, bougainvillea climbed, gloriously pink, between the white and blue.

"It's beautiful," she whispered, choking up. "I never imagined anything could be so beautiful."

"I can," Leonidas said huskily, looking down at her. He roughly pulled her into his arms.

As he kissed her, Daisy felt the sun on her bare shoulders, the warm wind blowing against her dress and hair, and she breathed in the sweet scent of flowers and the salt of the sea. She felt her husband's strength and power and heat. He wanted her. He adored her.

Could he ever love her?

He'd told her once that he couldn't. But then, hadn't Daisy said the same after learning his true identity—telling him she could never, ever love him again?

And she'd been wrong. Because in this moment, as Leonidas held her passionately in this paradise, she felt her love for him more strongly than ever.

A voice chirped words in Greek behind them, and they both fell guiltily apart. Maria, the housekeeper, was smiling, holding a lunch tray. With an answering smile, Leonidas went to take the tray from her.

"We'll have lunch at the table," he murmured to Daisy.

The two of them spent a pleasurable hour, eating fish and Greek salad and freshly baked flatbreads, along with briny olives and cheeses. It was all so impossibly delicious that when Daisy finally could eat no more, she leaned back in her chair, looking out at the sea, feeling impossibly happy.

She looked at her husband. As he gazed out at the blue water, his darkly handsome face looked relaxed. Younger. He seemed...different.

"Do you have any drawing paper?" Daisy asked suddenly. He turned to her with a laugh.

"Why?"

"I want to draw you."

"Right now?"

"Yes, now."

He went inside the villa, and a moment later, came back with a small pad of paper and a regular pencil. "It's the best I could find. It's not exactly an art studio in there."

"It's perfect," she said absentmindedly, taking it in hand. She looked at him as he sat back at the small table on the terrace. "Don't move."

He shifted uneasily. "Why are you drawing me?"

How could she explain this strange glow of happiness, this need to understand, to hold on to the moment—and to him? "Because...just because."

With a sigh, he nodded, and sat back at the table. As Daisy drew, she focused completely on line and shadow and light and form. Silence fell. He sat very still, lost in his own thoughts. As Leonidas stared at the villa, his relaxed expression became wooden, even haunted. To draw him back out, she prodded gently, "So you grew up here?"

"Yes." If anything, he looked more closed off. She tried again.

"You must have at least a few good memories of this place."

"I have good memories of Maria. And the hours I spent on this terrace. As a boy, I used to look out at the water and dream about jumping in the sea and swimming far, far away. Not stopping until I reached North America." The light slowly came back into his eyes. "The village is nice. The food. The people. I was free to walk around the island, to disappear for hours."

"Hours?" She lifted her eyebrows, even as she focused on the page. "Your parents didn't worry?"

"They were happy I was gone."

Moving the pencil across the white page, Daisy gave a snort. "I'm sure that's not true..." Finishing the sketch, she held it up to him with quiet pride. "Here."

Reaching out, Leonidas looked at the drawing. Daisy smiled. It was the best thing she'd done in ages, she thought. Maybe ever. He looked younger in the drawing, happy.

He touched the page gently, then whispered, "That's how you see me?"

"Yes." She'd drawn him the way she saw him. With her heart.

Silence fell, a silence so long that it became heavy, like a dark cloud covering the sun. Then Leo roughly pushed the drawing back to her.

"You've got me all wrong," he said in a low voice. "It's time you knew." He lifted his black eyes. "Who I really am."

CHAPTER EIGHT

THIS WAS A MISTAKE. A huge mistake.

Behind him, Leonidas could hear the roar of the sea—or maybe it was his heart. He looked at Daisy, sitting across from him at the table.

His wife's eyes were big and green, fringed with dark lashes, and her full pink lips were parted. Her honey-brown hair fell in waves against her bare shoulders, over the thin straps of her white sundress. Behind her the magnificent white villa reached up into the blue sky, with brilliant pink flowers and green leaves along the white wall.

For the last few days, he'd tried to convince himself he was going to tell her everything, as he'd promised. She was his wife now. She was having his baby. If he couldn't finally let down his guard with her, then who?

Then he remembered how he'd felt when that gray-haired artist—Franck Bain—had burst in on their wedding and tried to take Daisy from him.

Don't marry him. He's a liar who killed your father—an innocent man.

If the security guards hadn't rushed the man out, Leonidas might have throttled Bain himself. Since the wedding yesterday, the man had been politely warned to leave New York. *Politely* might be an exaggeration. But he had left for Los Angeles and with any luck, they'd never see him again.

But Bain had been right about one thing. Leonidas was a liar. Not about Daisy's father, who hadn't been innocent in the forgery scheme.

But about himself.

For Leonidas's whole life, he'd lied about who he was.

He was tired of pretending. He wanted one person on earth to know him, really know him. And who could be more trustworthy than Daisy?

He wanted to tell his wife the truth. But the idea was terrifying. Even as he'd held his new bride, snuggled up against him, on the overnight flight from New York, tension had built inside him.

So he'd promised himself that he'd tell her at the *end* of their honeymoon, after a week of lovemaking, eating fresh seafood and watching the sun set over the Aegean.

Appearance is what matters. How many times had his parents drilled that into him as a child—not just by words, but by example? At twenty-one, he'd thrown himself into the luxury business, determined to do even better than Giannis and Eleni Niarxos had in projecting an aura of perfection. Leonidas had become his brand—global, wealthy, sophisticated, cold.

Except there was this quiet voice inside him, growing steadily harder to repress, that he was more than his brand, so much more. He wasn't the monster his parents had called him; he could be warm and alive. *Like her.*

Daisy licked her delicious pink lips. "What do you mean?" she said haltingly, her voice like music. "I don't know who you are?"

In her arms, pressed against her breasts and belly, she cradled her sketch of him.

It was the sketch which had made him blurt out the words. The man in her drawing looked strong and warm and kind and sure, with humor gleaming from his eyes. Nothing like Leonidas had ever been. Not even as a boy.

But perhaps he could still become that man if—

"Leo?"

"I was never meant to be born," he said. "My very existence is a lie." He gave a grim smile. "You might say I'm a forgery."

"What are you talking about?"

Leonidas took a deep breath. "You think I'm Leonidas Gianakos Niarxos, the son of Giannis Niarxos."

Her lovely face looked bewildered. "Aren't you?"

This was harder than he'd thought. He could not force the words from his lips. His whole body was screaming *Danger!* and telling him to be quiet before it was too late, before he risked everything.

Rising from the chair, he paced the wide terrace. He felt her eyes follow him. He probably looked crazy. Because he was. Keeping this story buried inside him for so long had made him crazy.

Turning, Leonidas gripped the railing of the balustrade, looking out at the sea beneath the hot Greek sun. "My parents married for love." He paused. "That was unusual for wealthy Greek families at the time. And they were young. My father was heir to the Niarxos company, which made luxury leather goods. My mother was the heiress to a shipping fortune. She brought money as her dowry—and a Picasso."

"Love with Birds," Daisy whispered, then cut herself off.

"Yes." He glanced back at her. "From everything I've heard, my parents were crazy about each other." His hands tightened. "But years passed, and they could not have a baby. Society's golden couple was not perfect after all. All of their friends, who'd been secretly jealous of their flaunted passion, taunted them with their smug pity. And when it turned out to be my father's fault that they could not conceive, my mother started complaining about him to her friends. Their love evaporated into rage and blame." He glanced back at her. "I only heard of this years later, you understand."

Daisy's face was pale. "Then you were born..."

"Right." Leonidas gave a crooked smile. "Nine months later, I was born. Their marriage was saved. And that was the end of it."

Setting down her sketchbook carefully on the table, she rose to her feet. Going to him on the edge of the terrace, she said quietly, "What really happened?"

His heart was pounding painfully beneath his ribs. "I'm the only one alive," he whispered, "who knows the full story."

Leonidas looked down at the pounding surf on the white sand beach below.

"From the time I was born, everything I did or said seemed to set my father on edge, making him yell that I was useless and stupid. My mother just avoided me. It was only at fourteen, after my father's funeral, that I learned the reason why."

Standing beside him, Daisy didn't say a word.

"I always had the best clothes, the best education money could buy. *Appearance* was what mattered to them. No one must criticize how they treated their only child." He paused. "If not for Maria, I'm not sure I would have survived."

Reaching out, she put her hand over his on the railing. "Leo..."

Leonidas pulled his hand away. He couldn't bear to be touched. Not now. Not even by her. "I knew something was wrong with me. I could not please them, no matter how I tried. Something about me was so awful that my own father and mother despised me. And though everyone in Greece seemed to think my parents still had this great love affair, at home, they ignored each other—or threw dishes and screamed. Because of me."

"Why would you blame yourself for their marriage problems?"

For a moment, he fell silent. "I heard them sometimes, arguing at night, when I was home during school holidays." He glanced back at the villa. "This is a big house. But sometimes they were loud. One of them always seemed to be threatening divorce. But neither was willing to give up the Picasso. That was the sticking point. Custody of the painting. Not me."

Her stricken eyes met his.

Leonidas paused, then said in a low voice, "When I asked if I could stay at my boarding school year-round, they agreed. Because they could tell other people they'd only done it to make me happy. Appearance was all that mattered to them. My parents stayed together in their glamorous, beautiful lives, pretending to be happy."

"How could they live like that?"

"My father quietly drank himself to death." His

lips twisted upward. "When I came home to attend his funeral, I was shocked when my mother hugged me, crying into my arms. I was fourteen, still young enough to be desperate for a mother's love." Leonidas still hated to remember that rainy afternoon, as he'd stared at his father's grave, and his mother, dressed all in black, had embraced him. "I thought maybe she needed me at last. That she…loved me." He gave a bitter smile. "But after the service was over, and her society friends were gone, my mother stopped pretending to be grief stricken. She calmly told me that she was leaving me in the care of trustees until I inherited my father's estate. She was moving to Turkey to be with her lover. She said there was no reason for us to ever see each other again."

"What?" Daisy cried. "She said that? At your father's funeral? How could she?"

He gave a low laugh. "I asked her. *Why, Mamá? Why have you always hated me? What's wrong with me?*" His jaw tightened. "And she finally told me."

Silence fell on the villa's terrace. Leonidas heard the wind through nearby trees, ruffling the pages of his wife's sketchbook on the table.

"My father had been enraged at my mother telling their friends that it was his fault they couldn't conceive, that he wasn't *a real man*. He wanted to shut her up—and go back to being the golden couple of society." He narrowed his eyes.

"He had a brother, Dimitris, his identical twin, a few minutes younger. My grandfather had cut off Dimitris without a dime for his scandals, leaving him nothing to buy drugs with. Until my father came to him with an offer—asking him to make love to my mother in the dark and cause her to conceive a child without realizing that the man impregnating her wasn't my father." He paused. "My uncle agreed. And he succeeded."

"What are you saying?"

"My uncle was my real father." Leonidas took a deep breath. "I never knew him. Before I was born, he burned himself out in a blaze of drugs. My father had believed that after I was born, he'd be able to forget he wasn't my real father. After all, biologically I would be, or close enough. But he couldn't forget that his brother had made love to his wife. And he couldn't forgive her for not noticing the difference. Shortly after I was born, when my mother lashed out at him for ignoring their new baby, he exploded, and called her a whore."

Daisy's face was stricken. "Oh, Leo…"

"She forced him to explain. After that, she couldn't forgive what he'd done to her, that she'd made love to her drug-addicted brother-in-law without knowing it. Her own husband had tricked her. Every time she looked at her newborn baby— *me*—she felt dirty and betrayed."

Tears welled in her eyes. "But it wasn't your fault—none of it!"

He took a deep breath, looking up bleakly as plaintive seagulls flew across the stark blue sky. "And yet, it all was."

"No," Daisy whispered.

"Appearance is what matters," he said flatly. "Giannis wasn't really my father, and my parents despised each other. But to the outside world, they pretended they were in love. They pretended they were happy." He paused. "They pretended to be my parents."

Tears were streaking Daisy's cheeks.

"When my mother said there was no need for us ever to see each other again, right after she'd just been hugging me and crying in my arms, something snapped. And... And..."

"And?"

Leonidas took a deep breath. "I saw her Picasso, sitting nearby, waiting to be wrapped and placed in a crate. Something in my head exploded." He looked away. "I grabbed some scissors from a nearby table. I heard my mother screaming. When I came out of my haze, I'd slashed the entire side of *Love with Birds*, right across its ugly gray heart."

He exhaled. "My mother wrenched the scissors out of my hands, and told me I was a monster, and that I never should have been born." He looked back at Daisy. "Those were her last words to me. A few weeks later, she died in the Turkish earthquake. Her *yali* was smashed into rubble and rock. Her body was found but the painting was lost."

"So that's how you knew the Picasso was a fake," Daisy whispered, then shook her head. "And no wonder you wanted it so badly. No wonder you were so angry when…" She swallowed, looking away.

Looking down, he said thickly, "After I became a man, I thought if I could own the painting, maybe I would understand."

"Understand what?"

"How they could love it so much, and not—" His throat closed.

"Not you," she whispered.

His knees felt like rubber. He couldn't look at her. Would he see scorn in her eyes? Or worse— pity?

He'd grown up swallowing so much of both. Scorn from his family. Pity from the servants. He'd spent his whole life making sure he'd never choke down another serving of either one.

But he was about to become a father. His eyes fell to Daisy's belly, and he felt a strange new current of fear.

What did he know about being a parent, with the example he'd had? What about Leonidas— either as a desperate, unloved boy, or an arrogant, coldhearted man—had made him worthy to raise a child?

"Leo," Daisy said in a low voice. With a deep breath, he met her gaze. His wife's eyes were shining with tears. "I can't even imagine what you went through as a kid." She shook her head. "But that's all over. You have a real family now. A baby who will need you. And a wife who… who…" Reaching up, she cupped her hands around his rough jawline and whispered, "A wife who loves you."

Leonidas sucked in his breath, his eyes searching hers. Daisy loved him? After everything he'd just told her?

"You…what?"

"I love you, Leo," she said simply.

His heart looped and twisted, and he couldn't tell if it was the thrill of joy or the nausea of sick terror.

"But—how can you?" he blurted out.

Her lovely face lifted into a warm smile, her green eyes shimmering with tears. "I've always loved you, from the moment we met. Even when I tried not to. Even when I was angry… But I love you. You're wonderful. Wonderful and perfect."

She loved him.

Incredulous happiness filled his heart. On the villa's white terrace, covered with pink flowers and overlooking the blue sea, Leonidas pulled her roughly into his arms, and kissed her passionately beneath the hot Greek sun.

Hours later, or maybe just seconds, he took her hand and led her inside the villa, to the vast master bedroom, with its wide open windows overlooking the Aegean.

Taking her to the enormous bed, he made love to her, as warm sea breezes blew against gauzy white curtains. He kissed her skin, made her gasp, made her cry out her pleasure, again and again.

Much later, when they were both exhausted from lovemaking, they had dinner, seafood fresh from the sea, along with slow-baked lamb marinated in garlic and lemon, artichokes in olive oil, goat's milk cheese, salad with cucumber and tomatoes, and freshly baked bread.

Full and glowing, they changed into swimsuits and walked along the white sand beach at twilight, as the water rolled sensuously against their legs. They stopped to kiss each other, then chased the waves, laughing as they splashed together like children in the turquoise-blue sea, the sunset sky aflame.

Leonidas watched her, the way she smiled up at him, her eyes so warm and bright. Daisy glowed like a star, her wet hair slicked back, the white bathing suit clinging to her pregnant body. His heart was beating fast.

I love you, Leo.

The setting sun was still warm on his skin as he came closer in the water. She looked at his intent face, and her smile disappeared. Taking her hand, he led her back to the villa, neither of them speaking.

Once they reached the bedroom's en suite bathroom, he peeled off her swimsuit, then his own. He led her into the shower, wide enough for two, and slowly washed the salt and sand off their bodies.

Drawing her back to the enormous bed, he made love to his wife in the fading twilight, with the dying sun falling to the west, as the soft wind blew off the pounding surf. In that moment, Leonidas thought he might die of happiness.

I love you.

For the first time in his life, he felt like he was home, safe, wanted, desired. He and Daisy were connected in a way he'd never known, in a way he'd never imagined possible. Their souls were intertwined, as well as their bodies. *She loved him.* As he held her in the dark bedroom, he knew he'd never be alone again. He could finally let down his guard—

His eyes flew open.

But what if Daisy ever *stopped* loving him?

He felt a sudden vertigo, a sickening whirl as the earth dropped beneath him. He didn't think he could survive.

But how could he make sure her love for him

endured, when he had no idea why, or *how*, she could love him? Even his own mother had said Leonidas should never have been born. Whatever Daisy might say, he knew he wasn't good enough for her.

And as for being good enough for their child...

Stop it, Leonidas told himself desperately, trying to get back to the perfect happiness of just a moment before. Squeezing his eyes shut, he held Daisy close. He kissed his wife's sweaty temple, cradling her body with his own.

It was a perfect honeymoon. When they returned to New York a few days later, Leonidas vowed that Daisy would never regret marrying him. If he could not feel love for his wife in his cold, ashy heart, he would at least show her love every day through his actions.

And for the first three months of their marriage, she did seem very happy, as they planned the nursery, went to the theater and even took cooking and baby prep classes together. Leonidas felt like a fool as he burned every type of food from Thai to Tuscan, no matter how hard he tried.

In order to spend his days—and nights—with her, he ignored work, and did not regret it. Even when Leonidas did go in to the office, instead of focusing on sales throughout his global empire, he found himself asking his employees random questions about their lives, as Daisy did. For the first time, he was curious about their families, their goals and what had brought them to work at Liontari.

His vice presidents and board members obviously thought Leonidas was lost in some postnuptial sensual haze. But they forgave him, because the explosive global reaction to his wedding to the daughter of the man he'd sent to prison had caused brand recognition to increase thirty percent. Leonidas and Daisy had had calls for interviews on morning shows, and even four calls from Hollywood, offering to turn their story into a "based on a true story" movie. Daisy had been horrified.

Leonidas had been happy to refuse. He'd discovered to his shock that he was happy working fewer hours. His heavily pregnant wife wanted him at home. She *needed* him at home. How could profit and loss reports compare with that?

But everything changed the day their baby was born.

On that early day in June, when the flowers were blooming outside the modern hospital in New York and the sky was the deepest blue he'd ever seen, Leonidas finally held his sweet tiny sleeping baby in his arms.

The newborn fluttered open her eyes, dark as his own. Her forehead furrowed.

And then, abruptly, she started to scream, as if in physical pain.

"She's just hungry," the nurse said soothingly.

But Leonidas was clammy with sweat. "Here. Take her. Just take her—"

He pushed the shrieking bundle into his wife's welcoming arms. Holding their daughter in the bed, Daisy murmured soft words and let the rooting baby nurse. Within seconds, the hospital suite was filled with blessed silence. Daisy smiled down at her baby, touching her tiny fingers wonderingly. Then she looked up at Leonidas.

"Don't take it personally," she said uncertainly.

"Don't worry," he ground out. But Leonidas knew it was personal. His own daughter couldn't stand to be touched by him. Somehow, the newborn had just known, as his parents had, that Leonidas was not worthy of love. Though Daisy's kind heart had momentarily blinded her to his flaws, her love for him would not last. And it would not save him.

He was on a ticking clock. Any day now, she would realize what their baby already knew.

And by the end of the summer, his prophecy came true. As weeks passed and Leonidas refused to hold the baby again—for her own sake—he watched with despair as his wife's expression changed from bewilderment to heartbreak, and finally cold accusation.

It was the happiest day of Daisy's life when their baby was born in the first week of June.

At least, it should have been.

Labor was hard, but when it was over, she held her little girl for the first time. She looked up at her husband, wanting to share her joy.

But for some reason, his handsome face was pale, as if he'd just seen a ghost.

Their baby was perfect. Little hands, little feet, a scrunched-up beautiful face. They named her Olivia—Livvy—after Daisy's mother, Olivia Bianchi Cassidy. Daisy was nervous, but thrilled to bring her back to the brownstone that had somehow become home to her, to the sweet pink nursery she and Leonidas had lovingly prepared.

It was hard to believe that was two months ago. Now, as Daisy nestled her baby close, nursing her in the rocking chair, she couldn't get over how soft Livvy's skin was, or how plump her cheeks had become in nine weeks. The baby's dark eyelashes fluttered as she slept. Her hair was darker than Daisy's, reflecting her namesake's Italian roots, as well as Leonidas's Greek heritage.

"Come and look at your daughter," she'd said to him more than once. "Doesn't she look like you?"

And every time, Leonidas would give their newborn daughter only the slightest sideways glance. "Yes."

"Won't you hold her?" she would ask.

And with that same furtive glance at his daughter, her husband would always refuse. Even if Daisy asked for help, saying she needed to have her hands free to do something else, like start the baby's bath, even *then* he would refuse, and would loudly call for Mrs. Berry to assist, as he backed away.

Leonidas disappeared from the house, claiming he was urgently needed at work. He started spending sixteen-hour days at the office and sleeping in the guest room when he came home late.

He claimed he did not want to disturb Daisy and the baby, but the end result was that Daisy had barely seen her husband all summer. He'd simply evaporated from their lives, leaving only the slight scent of his exotic masculine cologne.

For weeks, Daisy had felt heartsick about it. Obviously, their daughter wasn't to blame. Livvy was perfect. So it must be something else.

Back in March, during their honeymoon, when he'd told her about his tragic, awful childhood, it had broken Daisy's heart. But it had also given her hope. Some part of Leonidas must love her, for him to be so vulnerable with her.

And so she'd been vulnerable, too. She'd told him she loved him.

For months after that, Leonidas had held her close, made love to her, made her feel cherished and adored. He'd let her draw his portrait in six different sketches, all of them in different light.

Now she felt like those sketches were all she had of him.

Had there been a shadow beneath his gaze, even then? Had he already been starting to pull away?

In the two months since Livvy's birth, Daisy hadn't had the opportunity to do another drawing of Leonidas. But she'd done dozens of sketches of their baby. Looking through them yesterday, she'd been astonished at how much the infant had changed in such a short time.

Mrs. Berry, seeing the sketches, had shyly asked if she could hire Daisy to do her portrait, too, as a gift for her husband's birthday. Daisy had done it gladly one afternoon when the baby was sleeping, without charge. She'd done the drawing with her yellow dog stretched out over her feet, on the floor. Sunny had grown huge, and was always nearby, as if guarding Daisy and the baby from unknown enemies. She was particularly suspicious of squirrels.

Sunny always made her laugh.

Mrs. Berry had loved the drawing. Word of mouth began to spread, from the house's staff, to their families. Friends who came from Brooklyn to see the baby saw the drawings of Livvy, and requested portraits of their own grandchildren, of their spouses, of their pets. Just yesterday, Daisy had gotten five separate requests for portraits. She didn't know what to think.

"Why weren't you doing drawings like this all along?" Her old boss at the diner, Claudia, had demanded earlier that week. "Why were you doing those awful modern scribbles—when all along you could do pictures like this?"

Remembering, Daisy gave a low laugh. Trust her old boss not to be diplomatic.

But still, it made her think.

When she'd done her painting at art school, long ago, she'd been desperate to succeed. Art had always felt stressful, as she'd tried to guess what others would most admire. Each effort had been less authentic than the last, a pastiche of great masterpieces, as Leonidas had said. The painting her husband had bought at the auction for a million dollars was still buried in a closet. In spite of its success that night, she hadn't felt joy creating it. In spite of all her effort, the painting had never connected with her heart.

But these sketches were different. They were of *people*.

It felt easy to simply draw her friends—even new friends she'd just met—and see what was best in them.

Was it possible that Daisy did have some talent? Not for painting—but for *people*?

With a rueful snort, she shook her head. Talent for people? She couldn't even get her own husband to talk to her! Or hold their baby daughter!

Two days ago, heartsick, she'd been thinking of how, as an agonized fourteen-year-old, Leonidas had struck out at the Picasso with scissors. And she'd had a sudden crazy idea.

What if she found the painting for him?

It was a long shot. He'd been looking for it for decades. But maybe he hadn't been doing it the right way. Daisy had a few connections in the art world. If she could give him his heart's desire, would it bring Leonidas back to them?

It was her best chance. A grand gesture Leonidas would never forget. She pictured his joyful face when she presented him with the Picasso. Then he would take her in his arms and tell her he loved her.

Her heart yearned for that moment!

So she called a young art blogger she knew in Brooklyn. Aria Johnson had a huge social media following and a ruthless reputation. The woman was like a bloodhound, searching out stories about priceless art and scandals of the rich and famous. Even Daisy's father had been a little afraid of her.

Picking up the phone, she called her and told Aria haltingly about her husband's history with the lost Picasso.

Daisy didn't explain *everything*, of course. She didn't say a word about the way he'd been conceived. *That* was a secret she'd take to the grave. She just told her that *Love with Birds* had been lost when Leonidas's mother had died in a big Turkish earthquake, some two decades before.

"Yeah. I know the story." The blogger popped her gum impatiently. "People have looked for that Picasso for twenty years. Wild-goose chase. Why else would your father have thought he could forge it?"

"He didn't—"

Aria cut her off. "They only found the woman's body. No painting." Daisy had flinched. *The woman* had been Leonidas's mother. "Other bodies were found, though. Her household staff. A young man who no one came forward to claim."

"Could you look into it?" Daisy said.

"A widow. With money. Hmm... Was she beautiful?"

"I guess so," Daisy replied. What difference did Eleni Niarxos's beauty make?

"Anything else you can tell me?"

She swallowed hard. It felt like breaking a confidence—but how else could she be sure it was the right painting? She said reluctantly, "There's a cut in the canvas. Someone sliced the painting with a pair of scissors."

"Someone?"

"Yes. Someone." Quickly changing the subject, Daisy said, "If you could find it, I'd be so grateful. And I'll pay you—"

"You can pay my expenses, that's it. I don't need a finder's fee. I just need to own the *story*. Deal?"

Daisy took a deep breath. It felt like a devil's bargain, but she was desperate. "Deal."

The art blogger paused. "If I find the painting, it might not have provenance."

Meaning, the painting might have been stolen. Which would make sense. How else could it have simply disappeared during the earthquake?

"I don't care," Daisy said. "As long as the Picasso is genuine. And I want the story of where the person found it."

Aria popped her gum. "Don't worry. I'll get the story."

That had been a few days ago. Now, holding her sleeping baby, Daisy was rocking in the chair in the nursery. It was late August, hot and sweaty summer in New York, but cool and calm inside their West Village mansion. She looked down at Livvy, softly snoring in her arms, in rhythm with the much louder snoring of the large dog snoozing at Daisy's feet.

"Soon," she whispered to her baby. "Aria will find it. And then your father will be home, and he'll realize at last that he's really, truly loved—"

The nursery door was suddenly flung open, hitting the wall with a bang. The dog jumped at her feet. Livvy woke and started wailing, then Sunny started barking.

Looking up at the doorway in shock, Daisy saw her husband, dark as a shadow. He was dressed in a suit, but his handsome face held a savage glower.

For a moment, in spite of her baby's wails, Daisy's heart lifted. Her husband had come home to her at last. Her body yearned for his embrace, for connection, for reassurance. A smile lifted to her lips.

"Leonidas," she breathed. "I'm so glad to see you—"

"Do you really hate me this much, Daisy?" His voice was low and cold. "How could you do it?"

"What?" she cried, bewildered.

"As if you didn't know." Leonidas gave a low, bitter laugh. "I should have known you would betray me. Just like everyone else."

CHAPTER NINE

THE WELCOMING SMILE on his wife's face fled.

She'd made such a lovely picture, snuggled in the rocking chair beside the nursery's window, holding their sleeping baby, with the floppy golden dog at her feet.

Now Daisy's beautiful face was anguished, the baby was wailing and Sunny was dancing desperately around Leonidas, wagging her tail, trying to get his attention.

He ignored the dog, looking only at his wife.

Turning away, she calmed the baby down, pulling out a breast and tucking her nipple into Livvy's tiny mouth as comfort.

It shouldn't have been erotic, but it was. Probably because he hadn't made love to her in months. Leonidas tried not to look. He couldn't let himself want her. He couldn't.

He forced himself to look away.

She'd hurt him. In a way he'd never thought he'd hurt again.

He never should have told her about his past. Never...

As the baby fell quiet, falling asleep with her tiny hand pressed against his wife's breast, Daisy finally looked up at him. Her green eyes narrowed.

"What do you mean, I betrayed you?"

Ignoring the dog still pressing against his knees, Leonidas glared back, but lowered his voice so as not to wake their child. "You spoke with Aria Johnson."

"Oh, that." She relaxed, then gave a soft smile. "I was trying to help. I know what the Picasso means to you, and I asked her to find it. I didn't think—"

"No, you *didn't* think, or else you wouldn't have told a muckraking *blogger* that I cut into the painting with a pair of scissors!"

"What?" she gasped. "I never told her it was *you*!"

"Well, she knows. She just called me at the office. And if that weren't enough she's been looking into my mother's past," he said grimly.

Daisy went pale. She whispered, "What did she find?"

"My mother apparently had many lovers, both in Greece and Turkey. She tracked them all down, except for her last one, who apparently died with her in the earthquake." He glared at Daisy. "One of the lovers knew how I was born. My mother must have confessed. So now that blogger knows I'm not really my father's son, but the son of my drug-addicted uncle. She asked me to confirm or deny!"

"What did you say?" Daisy cried.

"I hung up the phone!" Clawing back his hair, Leonidas paced the nursery. Every muscle felt tense. "How could you have told her to look into my past?"

"I didn't! I just told her to find the Picasso!"

He looked down at her, his heart in his throat. "Aria Johnson has a reputation. She can't be bought off. All she cares about is entertaining her army of followers with the most shocking scandal she can find. And she always finds them. This is going to be all over the internet within hours."

Daisy looked up at him miserably, her eyes glistening with unshed tears. "I'm so sorry. I was trying to help."

"Help? Now the whole world is going to learn my deepest, darkest secret, which I've spent a lifetime trying to hide." He clenched his hands at his sides. "I never should have trusted you."

"I'm sorry." She blinked fast, her face anguished. "I didn't mean to hurt you. I was trying to bring you back!"

"What are you talking about?"

"The day Livvy was born, you disappeared!" The baby flinched a little in her arms at the rise in her voice. With a deep breath, Daisy carefully got to her feet, then lifted Livvy into her crib. Gently setting down the sleeping infant, she quietly backed away, motioning for Leonidas to follow, Sunny at his feet. Closing the nursery door silently behind them, Daisy turned to face him in the hallway.

The window at the end of the hallway slanted warm light into the hundred-year-old brownstone, gleaming against the marble floors. The big golden dog stood between them, her tongue lagging, looking hopefully first at one, then the other.

"I need you, Leonidas," Daisy whispered. "Our baby needs you. Why won't you even hold her?"

A tumble of feelings wrenched though him. He couldn't let them burst through his heart, he couldn't. He said stiffly, "I held her."

"Just once, in the hospital. Since then, you've avoided her." Her eyes lifted to his. "You've avoided me."

His wife's stricken expression burned through him like acid. He turned away.

"Work has been busy. You cannot be angry at me for trying to secure our daughter's empire…" Then he remembered that Daisy didn't care about his business empire. It wasn't enough for her. And if that wasn't, how could Leonidas ever be? "I haven't been avoiding you."

The lie was poison in his mouth.

"Please," she said in a low voice. "I need you."

"You don't. You're doing fine. And Livvy is better off with you than with me."

"What is that supposed to mean?"

How could he explain that his baby daughter already knew he was no good? And from the pain and hurt in his wife's eyes, Daisy was rapidly learning the same thing, too. "It doesn't matter."

Reaching out, she put her hand on his arm. "You helped me love art again, after all my hope was lost. Drawing you on our honeymoon, I realized that people are my passion. Not random smudges or colors. *People*." Blinking fast, she tried a smile. "You helped me find my voice."

Daisy had never looked more beautiful to him than she did right now, her green eyes so luminous, her heart fully in her face.

And her love. He saw her love for him shining from her eyes. He didn't deserve it. He couldn't bear it. Because it wouldn't last.

His fate was in her hands, as he waited for Daisy to finally realize he wasn't worthy of her love. *You're wonderful*, she'd told him. *Wonderful and perfect.*

He wasn't. He knew his flaws; he could be cold and arrogant and selfish. But from the moment she'd decided to love him, she had become willfully blind. She had rose-colored glasses and was determined to see only the best of him.

But sooner or later she'd see the real him. Then her love would crumble to dust. To *disgust*.

Just the thought of that ripped him up.

And soon, the whole world would learn about his scandalous birth and not even his wealth or power would protect him. He'd done everything he set out to do. He'd built an empire. He was rich and powerful beyond imagination. But it had changed nothing.

All his worst fears were about to come true. The world would learn that his very birth had been a deceit. His parents had despised him and wished he'd never been born.

Leonidas was unlovable. Unworthy. Empty.

And now he was dragging Daisy into it as well.

"I'm sorry, Leonidas," she said quietly. "I never meant to hurt you. Can you ever forgive me?"

Shaking his head, he looked toward the window at the end of the hallway. If he had any decency, he would let both her and the baby go.

But just the thought of that made his soul howl with grief…

Daisy bit her lip. "Even if Aria publishes everything, why would anyone care? What does the way you were conceived have to do with you?"

He looked at her incredulously. "Everything."

She shook her head. "You had an awful childhood and triumphed in spite of it all. That's the *real* story, whoever your father was."

Leonidas didn't answer.

"Besides. You never know," she tried, "maybe the Picasso will be found…"

"It will never be found." He gave a low, bitter laugh. "It was buried beneath ten tons of rock and fire."

"But you said they never found it—"

"It must have been destroyed." Like so much else.

A long, empty silence fell between them in the hallway.

"Leonidas," she said quietly. "Look at me."

It took him a moment to gather the courage. Then he did. His heart broke just looking at her, so beautiful and brave, as she faced him, her shoulders tight.

"I'm sorry if I've caused you pain," she said quietly. "My desperation made me reckless." Her lovely face was bewildered. "You asked me to marry you. You *insisted* on marriage. You said there was nothing you wanted more than to be Livvy's father. What happened?"

"I don't know."

"If you're never going to hold her, never going to look at me—why are we married? Why am I even here?"

It was clear. He had to let them go. If he didn't, he'd only ending up hurting them so much more.

But how could he let them go, when they were everything?

Hurt them—or hurt himself. There was only one choice to make. But it hurt so much that Leonidas thought he might die. He looked around the hallway wildly, then gasped, "I need some fresh air—"

Turning, he rushed down the stone staircase and stumbled outside, desperate to breathe.

Outside the brownstone mansion, the tree-lined street was strangely quiet. The orange sun, setting to the west, left long shadows in the hot, humid August twilight. He stopped, leaning over, gasping for breath, trying to stop the frantic pounding of his heart.

Daisy came out of the house behind him, to stand in the fading light.

"I love you, Leonidas," she said quietly.

His hands clenched. Finally, he turned to face her.

"You can't."

"The truth is, I've always loved you, from the moment we met at the diner, and I thought you were just Leo, a salesclerk in a shop." Reaching up, she cupped his unshaven cheek. "I fell in love with you. And who you could be. And I only have one question for you." She tilted her head. "Can you ever love me back?"

Trembling beneath the shady trees of summer twilight, Leonidas closed his stinging eyes. He felt like he was spinning out of control, coming undone. But his heart was empty. He'd learned long ago that begging for love only brought scorn. The only way to be safe was to pull back. To not care.

The only way to keep Daisy and Livvy safe

from him, to make sure he never hurt or disappointed them, was to let them go.

He had to. No matter how much it killed him. He had to find the strength, for their sakes.

Closing his eyes, he took a deep breath.

Then he opened them.

"No. I'm sorry." He covered her hand gently with his own. "I thought I could do this but I can't."

"Do what?"

He looked down at her.

"Marriage," he said quietly.

Her eyes widened, her face pale. He pushed her hand away.

"No," she choked out. "We can go to counseling. We can—"

"You're in love with some imaginary man, not me. I'm not *wonderful*. I'm not *perfect*. I'm a selfish, cold bastard."

"No, you're not, you're *not*!"

"I am. Why can't you admit it?" he said incredulously. "Whatever you say, I know you've never forgiven me for killing your father."

"I have… I've *tried*." Tears were streaming down her face. "Dad was innocent, but I know now you never meant to cause his death."

"Stop." He looked at her, feeling exhausted. "It's time to face reality."

"The reality is that I love you!"

"You're forcing yourself to overlook my flaws.

But I've known from the moment Livvy was born that you'd soon see the truth, as she did from the first time I held her."

"Because she cried? That's crazy! She's a baby!"

"It's not crazy. You both deserve better than me. And I'm tired of feeling it every day, tired of knowing I'm not good enough. I'm not this perfect man you want me to be. Seeing the cold accusation in your eyes—"

"What are you *talking* about?"

"Better to end it now, rather than…" Turning away, he said in a low voice, "You and the baby should go."

"Go?" She gave a wild, humorless laugh. "Go where?"

"Anywhere you want. Your old dream of California."

"You're my dream! You!"

Every part of Leonidas's body hurt. He felt like he was two hundred years old. Why was she fighting him so hard? Why—when everything he said was true? "Or if you want, you can keep this house." He looked up at the place where they'd been so happy, the house with the ballroom where they'd quarreled and the garden where they'd played with the dog in the spring sunshine, where wild things grew in the middle of Manhattan. "I'll go to a hotel." He paused. "Forget what the prenup said. You can have half my fortune—half of everything. Whatever you want."

She looked up at him, tears in her eyes.

"But I want you."

"Someday, you'll thank me," he said hoarsely. It was true. It had to be true. He looked one last time at her beautiful, heartbroken face. "Goodbye, Daisy."

Squaring his shoulders, he turned away, walking fast down the quiet residential lane, filled with the soft rustle of leaves in the warm wind.

But even as he walked away, he felt her tears, her anguished grief, reverberating through his body, down to blood and bone.

It's better this way, Leonidas repeated to himself fiercely, wiping his eyes. *Better for everyone*.

So why did he feel like he'd just died?

Daisy watched in shock as her husband disappeared down the quiet lane in the twilight. At the end of the street, she saw him hail a yellow cab.

Then he was gone.

Once, long ago, she'd made Leonidas promise that if she ever wanted to leave, he had to let her go.

She'd never imagined he would be the one to leave.

All her love hadn't been enough to make him stay. He'd turned on her.

Yes, she'd blamed Leonidas once, for her father's unjust imprisonment and death. But she'd forgiven that, even if she hadn't forgotten it. Right?

Well. It didn't matter now.

Tears streamed down her face. Turning unsteadily, she stumbled back up the stoop to enter the house he'd just told her was hers. He'd given up the fifty-million-dollar brownstone easily, as if it meant nothing. Just like Daisy and their daughter.

If he'd cared at all, he never would have abandoned them. He would have tried to make their marriage work. Tried to love her.

But he hadn't.

Daisy closed the door behind her and leaned back against it. Above her, the crystal chandelier chimed discordantly in the puff of air.

The luxury of this mansion mocked her in her grief. This place was a palace. It was heaven. But it felt like an empty hell.

She stared blankly at the sweeping stone staircase where her husband had once carried her up to the bedroom, lost in reckless passion.

Her knees gave out beneath her and she slid back against the wall with a sob, crumpling onto the floor.

Her dog, coming downstairs to investigate, gave a worried whine and pushed her soft furry body against Daisy, offering comfort. She wrapped her arm around the animal and stared dimly at the opposite wall, where she'd framed sketches of her husband and baby.

"Mrs. Niarxos."

She looked up to see Mrs. Berry looking down at her with worried eyes. Swallowing, she whispered, "He left me."

"Oh, my dear." The white-haired housekeeper put her hand on Daisy's shoulder. Her voice was gentler than she'd ever heard before. "I'm so sorry."

The ache in Daisy's throat sharpened to a razor blade. "I thought, if I loved him enough…" Her image shimmered through a haze of tears. "I thought I could love him enough for both of us."

Mrs. Berry's hand tightened, and she said quietly, "I've known the boy for a long time. He never learned to love anyone. Least of all himself."

"But why wouldn't he? He's amazing. He's wonderful. He…" She heard the echo of his words. *I'm not wonderful. I'm not perfect. I'm a selfish, cold bastard.*

"What can I do, my dear?"

"I…" Shaking, Daisy closed her eyes. Still sitting on the marble floor, she gripped her knees against her broken heart. She couldn't imagine any future. All she saw ahead of her was a bleak wasteland of pain.

Then Sunny put her chin against Daisy's leg, her black eyes looking up mournfully, and Daisy remembered that she couldn't fall apart. She had a baby relying on her.

Five months ago, she'd thought she was ready to raise their baby alone. She'd made plans to go to nursing school, to move to California. She'd been strong in herself. She hadn't needed him.

Where had that strong woman gone?

She'd long since canceled her college registration. Daisy blinked fast, trying to see clearly. She stroked her dog's soft golden fur. She took a deep breath. Strong. She had to be strong.

She looked up at Mrs. Berry. "I need to go."

"Go?"

Daisy slowly got up. She looked around the elegant foyer. "I can't stay here. It reminds me too much of him. And how happy we were…"

The housekeeper gave her a strange look. "Were you really?"

Staring at her, Daisy held in her breath. Had they been happy?

"I thought we were," she choked out. "At least at first. But something happened when our baby was born…"

Across the foyer, Daisy's eyes fell again on the framed sketch she'd done of her husband on their honeymoon. They'd been happy then. Next to that, there was a framed sketch of their baby's smiling face and innocent dark eyes. Just like Leonidas's—and yet nothing at all like them.

With a deep breath, Daisy lifted her chin.

So be it.

Ahead of her, the empty future stretched as wide as a vast ocean.

She could fill that terrifying void with flowers and sea breezes.

"I need to pack," she said aloud, hardly recognizing the sound of her own voice.

By the next morning, Daisy, her baby and her dog were en route to California, in search of a new life, or at least a new place, where she could build new memories. And, she prayed, where she could heal and raise her daughter with love.

"We've found it, Mr. Niarxos."

Leonidas stared at his lawyer.

"No," he said faintly. "Impossible."

Edgar Ross shook his head. "I waited to be sure. We were contacted two weeks ago. It's been authenticated. There can be no doubt."

The two men were standing in his chief lawyer's well-appointed office, with its floor-to-ceiling windows and view of the Empire State Building.

When his lawyer had called him that morning, Leonidas had assumed that the man must have heard that he'd separated from Daisy. After all, for the last three weeks, Leonidas had been living in a Midtown hotel suite. It wouldn't exactly take a detective to figure out the Niarxos marriage was over.

Even though he'd told his wife to go, part of him still couldn't believe that Daisy and their baby had left New York. He'd returned to the mansion only once since she'd gone, and it had felt unbearably empty.

After that, he'd returned to the hotel suite, where he'd been riding out the scandal ever since the sordid truth about his past had been revealed on Aria Johnson's website, in all its ugly glory. This visit to his lawyer's office, on the thirty-fourth floor of a Midtown skyrise, was his first public outing in days. At least the scandal was starting to abate. Only two paparazzi had followed him here, which he took as a victory.

Misinterpreting his silence, his lawyer gave Leonidas a broad smile. "I don't blame you for being skeptical. But we really have found the Picasso."

"How can you be sure?" Leonidas's voice was low. "I don't want my hopes raised, only to have them crushed. I'd prefer to have no hope at all."

Just like his marriage.

He could still see Daisy's beautiful face in the warm Greek sun, surrounded by flowers on the terrace of his villa. *I love you,* she'd said dreamily. *You're wonderful. Wonderful and perfect.*

So different from her agonized, heartbroken face when, on the street outside their New York home, he'd told her he was leaving her.

Leonidas couldn't get those two images out

of his mind. For the last three weeks, he'd been haunted by memories, day and night, even when he was pretending to work. Even when he was pretending to sleep.

"Would you like to see your Picasso, Mr. Niarxos?"

Leonidas focused on the lawyer. He took a deep breath, forcibly relaxing his shoulders as they stood in the sleek private office with its view of the steel-and-glass city, reflecting the merciless noonday sun. "Why not."

With a big smile, the lawyer turned. Crossing the private office, he reached up and, with an obvious sense of drama, drew back a curtain.

There, on the wall, lit by unflattering overhead light, was the Picasso. There could be no doubt. *Love with Birds*.

Coming forward, Leonidas's eyes traced the blocky swirls of beige and gray paint. His fingers reached out toward a jagged line in the upper left corner, where the image was slightly off kilter, clumsily stitched back together. In the same place where he'd stabbed it with scissors, as a heartsick, abandoned fourteen-year-old.

"How did you find it?" he whispered.

"That art blogger found it. Aria Johnson. She found a relative of your mother's…er…last lover." He coughed discreetly. "A twenty-two-year-old college student in Ankara. He'd taken the painting to his aunt's house the day before he disappeared in the earthquake."

"Took it? Stole it, you mean."

"Apparently not. The young man told his aunt the painting was a gift from some rich new girlfriend. She never learned who the girlfriend was, and she had no idea the painting was worth anything. She only kept it because she loved her nephew."

Leonidas stared at him, barely comprehending.

After years of fighting tooth and claw to keep her husband from taking the painting from her, Eleni had simply *given it away*? To a young lover she barely knew? How? Why?

And then he knew.

His mother had been broken, too. Betrayed, heartsick, desperate for love.

The thought was overwhelming to him. So it wasn't just Leonidas who felt that way. His mother had taken young lovers and given away her biggest treasure. His father had quietly drunk himself to death. Did everyone in the world feel broken? Feel like they were desperate for love they feared they'd never find?

He looked at the jagged tear across the priceless masterpiece. Ross followed his gaze.

"Er…yes. The aunt tried to repair the cut with a needle and thread, out of respect for her nephew's memory." His lawyer flinched. "You see the result."

It took Leonidas a moment to even find his voice. "Yes."

"She nearly had a heart attack when Aria Johnson told her she'd been keeping a Picasso in her gardening shed for the last twenty years."

"How much does she want for it?"

"The art blogger told her she'd be a fool to take less than ten million. That seemed a reasonable price to me, since she could potentially have gotten even more at auction. So as soon as it was authenticated, I paid her."

"You're saying the painting's mine?"

"Yes, Mr. Niarxos."

Leonidas took another step toward the painting. With his parents now dead, there was no longer anyone to scream at him for trying to touch it. Reaching up, he gently stroked the roughly stitched edge where he'd once hacked into it.

"We will of course send it to be properly restored—"

"No. I'll keep it as it is." Drawing back his hand, Leonidas looked at the treasure he'd chased all his life. *Love with Birds*. Looking at the gray and beige boxy swirls, he waited for joy and love to fill his heart.

Nothing happened.

"I thought you might wish to arrange something with Liontari's PR department," the lawyer said behind him. "Let them do outreach on social media. This will make a nice end to the soap opera story currently making the rounds about your, *er*, origins. If there's one thing the public likes more than a scandal, it's a happy ending."

Barely listening, Leonidas narrowed his eyes, tilting his head right and left to get a better angle as he looked at the painting, waiting for happiness and triumph to fill his heart.

All his life, he'd chased fame and fortune, luxury and beauty. He'd chased this masterpiece most of all.

Why didn't he feel like he'd thought he would feel? This was the possession that was supposed to make him feel *whole*. This painting was supposed to be love itself.

But Leonidas felt nothing.

Looking at it, he saw neither love nor birds. He saw meaningless swirls and boxes of gray and beige paint.

He felt cheated. Betrayed. His hands tightened at his sides. This painting meant *nothing*.

"Sir?" His lawyer sounded concerned. "Is there a problem?"

Leonidas looked away. "Thank you for arranging the acquisition." The sharp light from the skyscrapers of the merciless city burned his eyelids. His throat was tight. "You will, of course, receive your finder's fee and commission."

"Thank you, sir," Ross said happily. When Leonidas didn't move, he said in a different tone,

"Uh…is there something else you wish to discuss, Mr. Niarxos?"

This was the moment to ask for his divorce to be set in motion. Leonidas had already been dragging his feet for too long. Just last week, when he'd stopped by his old house, hoping for a glimpse of his family, Mrs. Berry had told him Daisy had rented a cottage in California, three thousand miles away.

"Rented…a cottage?" he'd asked, bewildered. "I gave her this house!"

"She didn't want it without you," his housekeeper said quietly. "I'm sorry, sir. I'm so sorry."

He'd felt oddly vulnerable. "I'm the one who ended it."

"I know." The white-haired woman had given him a sad smile. "You hated for her to love you. How could she, when you can't love yourself?"

Hearing those awful, true words, Leonidas had fled.

He could never go back to that house or see Mrs. Berry again. Never, ever. He'd pay her off, put the house on the market—

"Ah. I was afraid of this," the lawyer said with a sudden sigh. Turning, he sat down behind his huge desk, and indicated the opposite chair. "Don't worry, Mr. Niarxos. We can soon get you free."

Still standing, Leonidas frowned at him. "Free?"

Edgar Ross said gently, "It's all over town

you've been living in a suite at the Four Seasons. But don't worry." He shook his head. "We have your prenup. Divorce won't be hard, as long as Mrs. Niarxos doesn't intend to fight it."

No, he thought dully. Daisy had already fought as hard as she could for their marriage. She would not fight anymore. Not now he'd made it clear there was no hope.

He'd lost her. Lost? He'd pushed her out of his life. Forever.

He looked up dully. In place of a loving, beautiful, kindhearted wife, he had a painting. *Love with Birds.*

"Sir?" Ross again indicated the leather chair.

Leonidas stared at it. All he had to do was sit, and he'd soon get his divorce. His marriage would be declared officially dead. He'd lose Daisy forever, and their child, too. Just as he'd wanted.

He could take the painting to join the rest of his expensive possessions, back at his empty house in the West Village, or any of his other empty houses around the world. Instead of love and legacy, instead of a family, he'd have the painting.

You hated for her to love you. How could she, when you can't love yourself?

Leonidas had never been worthy of Daisy's love. She'd called him wonderful. She'd called him perfect. He was neither of those things. No wonder he was scared to love her. Because the moment he did—

The moment he did, she'd see the truth, and he would lose her.

But he'd lost her anyway.

The thought made his eyes go wide. He'd sent her away because he was terrified of ever feeling that hollowness again in his heart, of wanting someone's love and not getting it.

But he loved Daisy anyway.

With a gasp, Leonidas stared out the window. A reflected beam from another skyscraper's windows blinded him with sharp light.

He loved her.

He was totally and completely in love with his wife. And he had been, from the moment he'd married her. No, before. From the moment he'd kissed her. From the moment she'd first smiled at him in the diner, her face so warm and kind, so beautiful and real in her waitress uniform—

Nice suit. Headed to court? Unpaid parking tickets? You poor guy. Coffee's on me.

Daisy always saw the best in everyone. Including him.

Leonidas looked again at the Picasso. The painting was not love. It could never fill his heart.

Only he could do that.

All these years, he'd blamed his parents for his inability to love anyone, including himself. And maybe it was true.

But sooner or later, a man had to choose. Would he bury himself in grief and blame, and die choking on the dirt? Or would he reach up his hands, struggle to pull himself up and out of the early grave, to breathe sunlight and fresh air?

Leonidas chose life.

He chose her.

"I have to go," he said suddenly.

"What?" His lawyer looked bewildered, holding a stack of official-looking papers on his desk. "Where?"

"California." Leonidas turned away. He had to see Daisy. He had to tell her everything, to fall at her feet and beg her to forgive him. To take him back. Before he'd even reached the door, he broke into a run.

Because what if he was already too late?

CHAPTER TEN

THE BOUGAINVILLEA WAS in bloom, the flowers pink and bright, climbing against the snug white cottage overlooking the sea.

After three weeks of living there, Daisy still couldn't get over the beauty of the quiet neighborhood near Santa Barbara. From the small garden behind her cottage, filled with roses and orange trees, she could see the wide blue vista of the Pacific. Looking straight down from the edge of the bluff, she could see the coastal highway far below, but the noise of the traffic was lost against the sea breezes waving the branches of cypress trees.

Looking out at the blue ocean and pink flowers, Daisy couldn't stop herself from remembering her honeymoon, when Leonidas had kissed her passionately, on the terrace of a Greek villa covered with flowers, overlooking the Aegean. Even now, the backs of her eyelids burned at the memory.

When would she get over him? How long would it take for her to feel whole again?

"So? Did you decide?"

Hearing Franck Bain's voice behind her, she turned with a polite smile. "No, not yet. I'm not even sure how long I'm going to stay in California, much less whether I'll open my portrait business here."

"Of course." The middle-aged artist's words were friendly, but his gaze roamed over her, from her white peasant blouse and denim capri pants to her flat sandals. The echo of her old boss's words floated back to her. *You know he's in love with you.*

No, Daisy thought with dismay. Franck was her father's old friend. He couldn't actually be in love with her.

Could he?

Franck had called her from his home in Los Angeles that morning, saying he'd heard she'd moved to Santa Barbara, just an hour to the north. He'd offered to drive up for a visit. Remembering how he'd burst in at her wedding, she'd been a little uneasy. But he'd explained smoothly, "My dear, I was just trying to keep you from making a big mistake. If you'd listened to me, you wouldn't be going through a divorce now."

Which was true.

Daisy *did* want to get to know Santa Barbara, and look at possible locations for a portrait studio. Living in New York, she'd never learned to drive. When Franck offered to drive her wherever she wanted, even putting a baby seat in the back of his car, how could she refuse? Didn't a person going through a divorce need all the friends she could get?

Divorce. Such an ugly word. Every day for the last three weeks, since she'd rented the snug cottage, she'd waited in dread for the legal papers to arrive.

But there was no point putting it off. Leonidas didn't want her. He didn't want Livvy. He was done with them. He didn't care how much he'd hurt them.

Maybe Franck had been right when he'd shouted out at her wedding that Leonidas was a liar who'd killed her father.

Because there was no mercy in her husband's soul. He'd had her father sent to prison for an innocent mistake. For Daisy's own innocent mistake of trying to help him find the Picasso, Leonidas had cut her and their baby out of his life—forever.

With a lump in her throat, Daisy looked at their sweet, plump-cheeked baby in the sunlight of the California garden. Three-month-old Livvy had fallen asleep in the car and was still tucked snugly into her baby carrier outside.

"Thanks for showing me some of your drawings," Franck said, smiling at her. He considered her thoughtfully. "You're very good at portraits."

"Thanks." She hoped he wasn't about to suggest that she do a drawing of *him*. She felt weary of his company, and a little uncomfortable, too.

The way Franck had looked at her all afternoon was definitely more than *friendly*. Ten minutes before, on their way back to her cottage, he'd invited her to dinner, "to discuss your business options." Yeah, right. She'd been relieved to say no. Thank goodness she had a dog waiting at the cottage who needed to be let out into the garden!

Now Sunny bounded around them happily, sniffing everything from the vibrant rose bushes to the cluster of orange trees, checking on baby Livvy like a mother hen, then running a circle around the perimeter of white picket fence.

The only thing the large golden dog didn't seem to like was Franck.

The dog had growled at him at first sight, when he'd arrived to pick them up in his car. Daisy had chastised her pet, and so Sunny had grudgingly flopped by the stone fireplace to mope. But even now, the normally happy dog kept her distance, giving him the suspicious glare she normally reserved for squirrels.

"Yes," Franck said, stroking his chin as he looked at Daisy. "You have talent. More than I realized. I wonder if…"

Oh, heavens, was he about to proposition her? "If what?"

"I've moved my business to California." His thin face darkened. "Your husband ran me out of New York."

That was news to her. "Leonidas? Why?"

He shook his head. "It doesn't matter. He'll soon be your ex." Franck smacked his lips—she could swear he did. "Your divorce will make you very wealthy."

The last thing Daisy wanted to do was discuss the financial details of her divorce with Franck Bain. She looked at his sedan parked on the other side of the picket fence, wishing he would leave already. "Um…"

"So obviously you won't need an income. But I wonder," his gaze swept over her, "if you might be interested in doing something with me. For pleasure."

Ugh. The way he said *pleasure* made her cringe. She responded coldly, "What are you talking about?"

He lifted a sparse eyebrow. "You could be part of something big."

"I'm sure you are involved in many big things. Don't let me keep you from them."

"There's a good market in lost masterpieces." He tilted his head slyly. "Especially old portraits."

Daisy stared at him. Unease trickled down her spine. Could he possibly mean…? "What market?"

"Don't pretend you don't understand." He grinned. "How do you think I got so rich? I help clients find the paintings they most desire."

Time seemed to stop beneath the warm California sunshine. "You mean…by creating them?"

Franck shrugged.

"It was you," she whispered. "All this time you said my father was innocent. But you knew he was guilty. You were his accomplice."

Franck shook his head scornfully. "How else do you think Patrick was able to stay home and take care of you after your mother died? *She* brought in the income. His gallery barely made a penny."

She said hoarsely, "I can't believe it…"

"Patrick refused my offer for years. Then he suddenly had to take care of a little kid by himself. He came to me, desperate. We agreed that I would paint, and he'd use his connections to sell the art. We did very well. For years." Franck's reptilian eyes narrowed. "Until he wanted to go for the big score, selling a Picasso. We never should have tried it."

"Why did you, then?" she said in a small voice.

He shrugged. "Your father was worried about you. You'd just flamed out as an artist. And he was sick of selling forgeries to the nouveaux riches. He wanted to leave New York. Move somewhere and start over."

Memory flashed through her, of the night she'd been crying over her failure to sell a single painting.

We could start over, her father had told her suddenly. *Move to Santa Barbara.*

What about your gallery, Dad?

Maybe I'd like a change, too. Just one more deal to close, and then...

Could he have possibly taken such a risk— done something so criminal—just because he couldn't bear to see his daughter cry? Guilt flashed through her.

She glared at Franck. "You sat through his trial every day and never admitted you were his accomplice. You let him go to prison alone!"

He rolled his eyes. "The Picasso was your father's idea. I was happy selling cheap masterpieces to suckers. Selling a Picasso to a billionaire? I never liked the risk." He scowled. "And then your husband ruined everything. I'd done a perfect copy of the Picasso. But I heard last week that Niarxos had chopped it up with a pair of scissors as a kid?" He glowered. "How was I supposed to know? Who *does* that?"

"Someone who's hurting," Daisy whispered over the lump in her throat. Her heart was pounding. The foundation of what she'd thought was true in her life was dissolving beneath her feet.

I didn't do it, baby, her father had pleaded. *I swear it on my life. On my love for you.*

Her father had lied. He'd told her what she

wanted to hear. What he'd desperately wanted her to believe.

But why had Daisy let herself believe it?

When her mother got so sick, her father had stopped spending time at the gallery, spending it instead at home with his beloved wife, and their young daughter. Yet somehow, his gallery had done better than ever. He'd hired more people. Instead of their family having less money, they'd had *more*.

Why hadn't Daisy ever let herself see the truth?

Because she hadn't wanted to see. Because she'd wanted to believe the best of her father. Because she'd loved him.

And she still loved him. She would have forgiven everything, if he'd just given her the chance...

"Why didn't Dad tell me?" she said brokenly.

Franck shook his head. "He said you had to believe the best of him, or he was afraid that you wouldn't survive."

"That *I* wouldn't survive?" she said slowly. She frowned. "That doesn't make sense. It..."

She had a sudden memory of her father trying to talk to her, the day he'd been questioned by the police.

Daisy, I've been arrested... He'd paused. *You should know I'm not perfect—*

Of course you are, Dad, she'd rushed to say.

You're perfect. The best man in the world. Don't try to tell me anything different.

Would he have told her then? If she hadn't made it clear she didn't want to know about his mistakes?

And Leonidas. It was true that she'd never totally forgiven him for what he'd done to her father. She'd tried to forget. She'd told him he was perfect. Because she loved him.

The men she loved had to be perfect.

I'm not wonderful. I'm not perfect. I'm a selfish, cold bastard, he'd told her. And she'd insisted he was wrong.

But he wasn't. Leonidas could be selfish. He could be cold. Why couldn't she admit that, and say she loved him anyway?

Rose-colored glasses were a double-edged sword. She'd believed in her father, believed in her husband. She'd boxed them in, pressuring them to live up to that image of perfection, an image no one could live up to for long.

No wonder Leonidas had fled.

She'd insisted on his perfection, as if he were a shining knight on a white charger. And when he'd finally shown his weaknesses, she'd betrayed him, by telling his secrets to some reporter.

The fact that the lost Picasso had been finally found, as she'd heard that morning in the news, did not absolve her. Her cheeks went hot with shame.

Leonidas had been right. She'd betrayed him.

"We could be partners, you and I." Speaking softly in the sunlit garden, Franck moved closer to her. "My hands aren't what they used to be, but I have connections now. Even if you don't need the money after your divorce, you could do the paintings just for fun." He cackled. "Old masters for suckers. Much more satisfying than sketching fat babies and dogs!"

Daisy jerked back, glaring at him. "I *like* fat babies and dogs!"

His forehead furrowed. Seeing rejection in her set jaw, he stiffened, scowling. "Fine." Then his pale blue eyes gleamed. "But you owe me. For all those months I took care of you." He gave an oily smile. "If you won't paint for me, I'll take payment in other ways—"

He grabbed her roughly. She tried to pull away. "What are you doing—don't!"

"Don't you think I deserve a little kindness," he panted, his long fingers digging into her shoulders, "for all those months I took care of you—"

She struggled desperately as he lowered his head. Before he could force a kiss on her, she screamed—

Then everything happened at once.

Her baby woke and started wailing in the baby carrier...

Her dog rushed toward Franck, showing her teeth with a growl...

Daisy lifted her knee up, hard and sharp, against Franck's groin, causing him to give a choked grunt, and release her...

And—

"Get the hell away from her!"

Leonidas's enraged, deep voice boomed behind her. As Franck was stumbling back from her blow, her husband was suddenly there, vengeful in his black shirt and trousers, his powerful body stepping in front of her. Daisy's mouth parted in shock as Leonidas punched the other man hard in the jaw, knocking him to the ground.

"Don't you dare touch her!"

"Leo," she whispered, wondering if she was dreaming.

His tall, muscular form turned anxiously. "Are you all right, *agape mou*? He did not hurt you?"

Rubbing her shoulders a little, she shook her head, her eyes wide. "I'm all right."

Leonidas exhaled with relief. He scooped up their crying baby, who immediately quieted, comforted in her father's arms. Then he drew Daisy close, searching her gaze intently with his own.

"I'm so sorry," he said in a low voice. "Can you ever forgive me?"

Daisy stared up at Leonidas's handsome face. His jaw was dark with five o'clock shadow, as if he hadn't had time to shave. His usually immaculate clothes were rumpled, as if he'd rushed straight from the airport. His black eyes were vulnerable, stricken.

"Can *I* forgive *you*?" she repeated, bewildered.

"Very touching," Franck snarled at them from the grass.

"Shut up," Daisy told him, at the same moment Leonidas said pleasantly, without looking at the man, "Another word, and I'll set the dog on you."

Their normally goofy, people-loving dog was, indeed, growling at the man threateningly.

As Sunny approached, Franck Bain scrambled back, flinging himself over the white picket fence into a tangle of rose bushes. Daisy heard his sharp yelp followed by swift footsteps. His car engine started with a roar, then he peeled off down the road.

"Sunny!" Daisy's blood was still up as she called her pet back into the middle of the garden. Kneeling into the soft grass, she petted her dog again and again, crooning, "Good girl!" as the dog's tail wagged happily.

"I couldn't understand why you got involved." Behind her, Leonidas's voice was low. "The first time you heard crying in an alley, I didn't know why you insisted on going to see what it was. It seemed better to ignore it."

Still kneeling beside her dog, Daisy turned her head. Her husband stood behind her, tall and broad shouldered. His handsome face was full of emotion.

"You insisted on taking care of the puppy, when you barely had enough money to take care of yourself. It was foolish." He took a deep breath, his dark hair gleaming in the sun. "Why try to save something abandoned? Something so un-loved and broken?"

She saw sudden tears in his black eyes.

"Now I understand," he whispered. "Because you did the same with me."

Daisy's lips parted. Rising to her feet, she reached for him. He pulled her into his powerful arms.

"Oh, my darling," Leonidas breathed into her hair, holding her close against his hard-muscled chest. "How can you ever forgive me for leaving you? I thought I could never be the man you needed me to be, and I couldn't bear to let you down. But I never should have run away like a coward..."

"Stop." Daisy put her hand on his rough cheek. "I was wrong about so much. All that time I blamed you for putting an innocent man in prison... Franck admitted that my father was guilty, all along. And I refused to see it. Because I needed my dad to be perfect." She lifted her gaze to his. "Just like I needed my husband to be per-fect. I'm so sorry."

"I would give anything to be perfect for you." Holding their precious baby in the crook of one arm, he looked intently into her eyes. "You deserve it, Daisy. But I knew I could never be. I could never be good enough to deserve your love."

She clung to him in her cottage's flower-filled garden, overlooking the wide blue Pacific. "But you can—you *are*—"

"I convinced myself that you and Livvy would be better off without me. But after you left, my soul was empty. Nothing mattered. Even when I finally acquired the Picasso—thanks to you—"

"I heard about that. Was it everything you dreamed of?"

Leonidas looked down at her. "I finally had it, this thing I'd been searching for half my life, and I felt *nothing*. It was just swirls of paint. And I realized that everything I'd ever feared had come true. I'd lost the love of my life, by being too proud and stupid when you tried to save me, by not being brave enough to risk my heart. Now the only thing I fear," he said quietly, "is that I've lost you forever."

Her lips parted. "What did you say? The love of your life?"

"I love you, Daisy." Leonidas looked from her to the small, drowsy baby still cuddled against his hard-muscled arm. "You and Livvy are my life." He took a deep breath. "And I'll spend the rest of that life trying to be perfect for you, trying to be whatever you need me to be—"

"No," she cut him off. His handsome face looked stricken. Reaching her hand up to his rough, unshaven cheek, Daisy said, "You don't need to be perfect, Leo. You don't need to do anything or change anything. I love you. Just as you are."

His dark eyes shone with unshed tears. Taking her hand in his own, he lifted it to his lips and kissed it passionately. *"Agape mou—"*

Sooner or later, we all learn the truth, Daisy thought later. The truth about others, the truth about ourselves. If you could be brave enough to face it. Brave enough to understand, and forgive, and love in spite of everything.

As her husband pulled her against his chest, into the circle of his arms, with their tiny baby tucked tenderly between them, and their dog leaping joyfully around their feet, he lowered his head and kissed her with lips like fire.

And Daisy really knew, at last, what love was.

It wasn't about rose-colored glasses or knights on white horses. It wasn't about being perfect. It was about seeing each other, flaws and all. Loving everything, the sunshine and shadow inside every soul. And not being afraid.

As Leo kissed her beneath the orange trees, with their feet in the grass and dirt, it was better than perfect.

It was real.

Leonidas looked out of the back window of their West Village mansion with dismay. Amid a snowy January in New York City, another foot of snow had fallen the night before.

In their yard, Sunny was leaping back and forth through the blanket of white, chasing a terrified-looking squirrel. Snow clung to their dog's golden fur, including her ears and eyelashes.

"This is a disaster," Leonidas groaned to his wife, who was watching from the breakfast nook.

She looked up at him tranquilly, turning a page of her book. "How so?"

"If we let her inside again, Mrs. Berry will kill us." He sighed. "Sunny will just have to live in the yard from now on. I'll build her a dog house."

"*You* will?"

"I'll hire someone," he conceded. "Because Sunny can never come back inside. She'd track snow and dirt all over the floors and make the whole house smell of dog."

"No, she won't," his wife said serenely, turning another page. "You're going to give her a bath."

He looked back with alarm. "Me?"

Daisy smiled. "Who better?"

Leonidas's eyes lingered on her. Even after a full night of lovemaking, his wife looked more desirable than ever, sitting at their breakfast table in a lush silk nightgown and robe, sipping black tea and reading a book, as baby Livvy, now seven months old, batted toys in a baby play gym on the floor.

Leonidas said with mock severity, "Do you

really think you can give me orders and I'll just obey? Like a pet?"

She looked up from her book, her pale green eyes limpid and wide, fringed with dark lashes. Tilting her head, she bit her pink lower lip. Her shoulders moved slightly, causing the neckline of her robe to gape, hinting at the cleavage of her full breasts beneath the silk. His heartbeat quickened.

"Fine," he said. "I'll give the dog a bath. Not because you asked me. Because I want to."

Her smile widened, and she turned back to her book, calmly taking another sip of tea. He watched her lips press enticingly against the edge of the china cup, edged with twenty-four-carat gold.

"Maybe we can have a little quality time later," he suggested.

Daisy looked at him sideways beneath her lashes. "Maybe."

Glancing at their innocent baby, who seemed to be staring at them with big brown eyes, drool coming from her mouth as she'd just gotten her first tooth, Leonidas sat down next to his wife at the table. "Maybe we can have a *lot* of quality time later."

Smiling, she put her hand on his cheek. "Maybe."

They'd been married for nearly a year, but for Leonidas, it felt like they'd just met. Every day, he felt a greater rush, a greater thrill, at the joy of being with her.

But at the same time, he felt safe. He felt adored. He felt...home.

In the four months since they'd returned to New York, many things had changed. Daisy had become the most in-demand portrait artist in the city, all the more celebrated because she took so few clients. "I'm already so busy with our baby, and you," she'd said. "I simply don't have time for more right now."

Who was Leonidas to argue? Whenever she was ready to become a full-time artist, he suspected Daisy would take over the world. He felt so proud to be her man. Especially since, as she often told him, he was the one who'd given her the courage, and inspiration, to draw again.

He was home more now, too. His company was in the process of hiring a new CEO, as Leonidas had decided to step back and merely be the largest shareholder. "I don't have time for more," he'd told his wife tenderly. "I'm already so busy with the baby. And you."

He was glad to be leaving the company in good shape. The shocking scandal of his birth, building on the soap-opera-like quality of his wedding and fatherhood—which had already gone viral on social media— had created so much outrageous publicity that Liontari's brands had all gone up an average of six percent, causing a huge leap in shareholder value. Even the story that, as a rebellious, heartsick teenager, Leonidas had chopped up his mother's Picasso with scissors when she abandoned him, somehow had added a darker, sexier edge to some of his more traditional brands. Even the most elite, art-loving clientele had forgiven Leonidas for it, after he'd donated the Picasso to a museum last month.

He'd once believed that if people ever learned the truth about him, they would destroy him with pitchforks and scorn. Instead, he'd become some sort of folk hero. He'd heard rumors of a tele-novela in development, based on his life.

People were complicated, he thought. Success could be fleeting. All you had to do was look at Franck Bain, once so successful, to see that. A week after the man had fled Daisy's rented cottage in California, he'd been arrested in Japan for trying to pass off a supposedly lost Van Gogh.

Leonidas shook his head. He couldn't pretend he regretted the man's imprisonment. He deserved it. Though Leonidas liked to believe he was a changed man, an understanding, loving person who would never think of taking vengeance on others, he was glad he didn't have to prove it with Bain.

And it left Leonidas free to move on with his life, to more important things, like spending time with his wife, his child and his friends. They were all that mattered. The people who loved him. He loved them, too. Daisy and Livvy most of all.

He looked down at his wife now as she sat at the kitchen table. She gave him a mysterious smile. He was intrigued.

"Are you hiding something from me?"

"Wouldn't you like to know."

"Yes," he whispered, leaning forward. Drawing his hand down her long dark hair, he moved his lips against her ear, soft as breath. "And you're going to tell me."

He felt her shiver beneath his touch. He ran his hands over the blush-colored silk, softly over her shoulders, to her back, to her full breasts...

Her *very* full breasts.

He blinked, then pulled back, his eyes wide as he searched his wife's gaze. "Are you... You're not..."

"Not pregnant? I'm not."

He exhaled, shocked by his own disappointment. He hadn't even been thinking about trying for another baby, not yet. After all, Livvy was only seven months old. Was he really ready for another baby in the house?

More mayhem. More chaos. More love.

Yes, Leonidas realized. Yes, he was. He wanted another baby. Or six. A large family, big enough for a football team—that sounded perfect.

But there was no rush. He'd just keep putting in the practice, intensely and passionately, every night in bed. A smile traced the edges of his lips. It was a tough job, but someone had to do it.

"It's all right," he said huskily, lowering his head toward hers. "We'll keep trying…"

Daisy put her hand on his chest, stopping him before he could kiss her.

"I'm not," her green eyes twinkled, "*not* pregnant."

His forehead furrowed as he searched her gaze. Then he sucked in his breath. "Not *not* pregnant?"

Daisy ducked her head, her smile suddenly shy. "It must have happened at Christmas. Maybe Christmas Eve. That time under the tree…"

"Agape mou," he said, dazzled with joy. Taking her in his arms, he kissed his wife passionately at the kitchen table. As he held her, he wondered what he'd done to deserve such happiness.

Then the dog door thudded loudly, and suddenly there was a large wet hairy dog between them, shaking water and snow all over the room, and their baby girl gurgled with laughter. As Daisy pulled back from her husband's embrace, her eyes danced as she laughed, too.

And Leonidas knew their joy would last forever. Their lives wouldn't be all laughter, for sure. But they'd build their future together, day by day, through snow and sun, rain and roses.

It would never be perfect. But it would be happy. Just like him. Once, he'd been lost. He'd been broken. But Daisy had loved him anyway. He'd learned the meaning of love from the woman who, in spite of his flaws, had given him her precious heart.

* * * * *

If you fell in love with
Penniless and Secretly Pregnant
you're sure to adore these other stories
by Jennie Lucas!

Chosen as the Sheikh's Royal Bride
Christmas Baby for the Greek
Her Boss's One-Night Baby
Claiming the Virgin's Baby

Available now!